Queen of Wilmette

Book 7 of The Queens of the Castle Series

U.M. Hiram

D2R Management Group, LLC

♦ DEDICATION ♦

*To those who turn their trials into triumphs,
pain into passion, and don't allow their past
circumstances or challenges to dictate the outcome
of an amazing life or future.*

<h1 style="text-align: center">♦ ACKNOWLEDGEMENTS ♦</h1>

First and foremost, I am grateful to God for allowing me to be on this life-changing literary journey. I am humbled to have been included in this amazing book series. It all began with the Kings and Knights of the Castle. Now, here are these phenomenal Queens.

Naleighna Kai, you are an amazing person and gifted editor. I am appreciative of your coaching, support, and most of all your heart. Thank you for all that you do. I didn't take it lightly that you trusted me to tell Vikkas and Milan's story.

Karen D. Bradley, you are such a force and I appreciate everything that you do for Tribe. Thank you for allowing me to include Daron and Cameron in Queen of Wilmette along with providing your keen eye for final edits.

D.J. Mitchell and Christine Pauls, thank you so much for your time and expertise with beta reading and line editing respectively. Marie McKenzie, thank you for the final beta read. I appreciate each of you ladies and your valuable insight.

J.L. Woodson, you are such a talent as a book cover designer and graphic designer. Thank you for continuing to raise the bar.

NK Tribe Called Success, I appreciate each and every one of you. Your encouragement, support and genuine love mean the world to me.

Chapter 1

Alarms from every corner of Second Chance Safe Haven's security areas blared and echoed throughout the building. The young man with a blend of fear and confusion etched in his face yanked on the side doors of the center trying to gain access. A state-of-the-art system had been installed with three dimensional cameras with artificial intelligence scanning capabilities. As Milan and her day staff were preparing to change shifts, the teenager had rushed up to the doors, looking over his shoulders as though being chased by someone or something, tears streaming down his cheeks.

"Help me, please," he screamed. In the distance, two jeeps were closing in on the young man's location. Both vehicles loaded with four armed occupants each.

Without a second thought, Milan ran to the East door with a member of the security staff right alongside her. As if by divine intervention, she'd been able to view everything on the security cameras. Instinctively, cries for help were on her radar and tugged at her heart strings. The center was built on the foundation of making a difference in the life of the country's disadvantaged and underprivileged youth, both young women and men.

"What's your name?" she asked in what she hoped was a soothing voice as soon as they pulled him safely inside the building.

Out of breath and perspiring so hard his drenched shirt was plastered against his pale skin, "Jonathan Reinhart."

Milan peered at him. "Jonathan, why are you in such a panic?"

Wiping his eyes with the back of a trembling right hand, he looked up at her, "They want me to fight to overthrow our government, I can't do that. I don't believe in their cause. So, I ran, my mother said I would be safe here."

Pausing, then taking a deep calming breath, Milan processed his words. "Who wants you to fight and for what cause?"

He tensed up and grew eerily quiet, self-preservation mode. She would have to take a different approach to get him to open up. Tonight, she'd make sure he was provided shelter. Tomorrow they'd find out more about this young man.

Once Milan made sure he was settled in a room and ate a meal of flatbread and minced lamb meat, she left him in the capable hands of her evening staff. At least two male employees were always on each shift to ensure safety and provide that extra layer of internal security.

Because of the work they did, neighboring countries sought to close down the center. Thankfully, they were under the protection of the Durabian government and Kings of the Castle. She'd be back the following day and put her social work training into play to start building trust with their unexpected new resident.

Thirty minutes later, Milan grabbed a bottled water from the second shelf of her fridge. After taking some time to breathe, she slid into a shower to release some of the tension that built up throughout the day. Briefly, she thought about the young man who had seemingly fought his way to get to the center for protection. At least that was his claim. Tonight, he would be safe until they could verify his story.

Standing on the master bedroom balcony, Milan looked out at the beautiful Durabian skyline from the second level of her home. The six bedroom, seven bath mini mansion was located in a gated community that housed a number of their Castle family members. Peacefulness surrounded her as she closed her eyes and breathed in the fresh, crisp air.

Her thoughts shifted to the decisions she was forced to make concerning Second Chance Safe Haven. The launch and operations of the center were her baby. Its ultimate goal was to provide services such as educational training and a shelter to the individuals who were housed inside the facility. They were on the borders near Nadaum and the United Arab Emirates, in a span of six months their clientele had grown beyond anything originally planned.

With all of the unrest happening in neighboring countries, there'd been an influx of teens looking for a secure place. Milan's mission was to help as many of them as possible. Her own personal experience fueled this passion because she knew all too well the feeling of abandonment. Her mind flashed back to the day that her mother kicked her out of the house.

"Better get you one of them dope boys, worry about schooling later," Pearline said.

Shaking in anger with balled up fists, Milan shot back. "Wasn't daddy one of those dope boys? When does he get out of prison? What's him being in prison done for you?"

Pearline's anger got the best of her, and she was standing inches away from her youngest daughter. "Are you sassing me?"

"Just stating facts. Grandma said the minute a woman puts her faith solely in a man to take care of her is when she gives up every ounce of her power."

"Well, Wonder Woman, lasso your little brown ass upstairs and pack your shit. How's that for power?"

Even though her aunt tried to step in and stop what was happening, Milan went upstairs to grab her belongings. The last words that she spoke before walking out of the door and never looking back were, "One day, Mama, you're going to need me."

Ironically, her siblings were having babies, failing in school, or participating in some form of illegal activities. Her mother didn't achieve her personal dreams and placed the blame on having children. Most of her anger was aimed directly at her youngest daughter who never landed in any type of trouble. Inhaling and then exhaling a deep breath, Milan let all those troubling memories escape her mind, at least momentarily.

Refocusing her energy on the current issues in Durabia, she put her gaze on the table occupied by her laptop, notepad, binder, and calculator. Working through the phases she'd implement along with costs for the additions to the center were a top priority. More rooms and valued added services for the teens, totally in compliance with Durabian customs, as well as increased staffing.

Once again, she took in the peaceful horizon, envisioning the changes and upgrades that would be implemented but her mind strayed to the political tight rope she walked as well. One of the advantages working in her favor is that the center was self-funded. They didn't need to depend on governmental financial support to operate, even though there were strict guidelines to follow. She was an American, connected to Durabian royalty through Vikkas, her high school sweetheart. Although the facility was kept under the radar, for obvious reasons, word seemed to be getting around about its existence. That could bring danger to their doorstep. And it came in a form that they weren't prepared to hand

Chapter 2

"Father, you know that I'm tempted to persuade my wife to temporarily shut down Second Chance Safe Haven," Vikkas said, though the prospect of doing so was going to be an uphill and downhill battle. Leaving America and a lucrative social services career was a huge, life changing decision that she made to be with the man that she loved. Milan put her heart and soul into improving the lives of disadvantaged young people.

Khalil, Vikkas, and Jai were situated around a solid wood, gold accented conference table nestled in the West wing of the Durabian palace that housed a majority of its offices. They awaited the in person and virtual arrivals of Sheikh Kamran along with the rest of the Kings and Knights, and Cameron who had been given "King" status. News coming out of Nadaum had been alarming, to the point it was time to accelerate their timeline for the security measures already underway.

Dark clouds hung over the normally bright clear skies of Durabia, signaling that a severe storm was approaching. One that would cause disaster to everything in its path - hurricane, tornado, or tsunami. No one knew exactly which direction and when it might surface because everything was eerily calm. Reckoning day was slowly approaching, and mayhem would follow. On a political front and in social unrest as well.

Khalil locked gazes with his son. "I understand. Where would that leave the young men and women who she currently helps? Her need to protect is as strong as mine, which has been a large part of our every day, purposeful life."

"Do you really think Milan would want to do that?" his brother, Jai, asked. "You know your wife is a strong-willed woman and the work she does is important. Based on everything she's been through in her childhood; the center has served as an avenue for her to change these young people's lives even more than what she was able to accomplish in the states."

Young teens were being recruited by the neighboring country to fight and act as rogue agents. Disgruntled relatives of Sheikh Kamran were credited with leading these unsavory efforts. They had been banished after a kidnapping that was slated to enslave his wife and children. A primary concern for the three men seated at the table was that Milan's center was now a main target due to the nucleus of her business serving disadvantaged youth, but also the fact she was connected to one of the men sitting at this very table.

Vikkas looked at both men absorbing their concerns. They made valid points and didn't make things easier or calm the small amount of anxiety felt about this entire situation. They'd left America to get away from the drama and foolishness brought on by political and social unrest. Now, here the couple was on foreign land having to deal with threats.

"Jai, I get that, and I don't discount any of it," Vikkas said. "Riddle me this. How did you feel when you battled with Temple's delusional ex-fiancé?"

"Brother, you know the answer to that because you were there," Jai answered in a sarcastic tone. "Murderous. I was ready to annihilate anyone who proposed danger to her and still would to this day. Hands down, no questions asked."

"Exactly my point." His gaze shifted to the man whose striking handsome features mirrored his own, and his twin. "And, Father, did you forget what you wanted to do to the Maharaj elders for all of the drama they caused at my wedding reception?" Vikkas tried to contain a smile at that hilarious gunslinger memory. "Even though you did finally take the high road."

"Actually, Cameron put two of them on their asses before Sandy could hand Roscoe to dad," Jai said laughing, while his brother almost spit out a mouth full of water.

Khalil nodded and tried to contain a chuckle but failed. "What your brother and I are trying to tell you is that Milan is no lightweight. Did you forget that she put a bullet in her own brother?" Everyone in attendance smiled at that one. The man deserved it for blackmailing her in the first place, but then took a step too far being greedy.

"And you still married her though," Daron said.

"I'm not in danger," Vikkas shot back. Inwardly reminding himself to never piss her off.

"Of course not, Seth deserved it after the stunt he tried to pull," he continued. "You know the saying about 'don't start none' and he clearly did. Didn't expect his sister to follow through with that threat though."

"I felt that," Daron chided.

"Felt what?"

"Those second thoughts floating through your mind."

"Whatever," Vikkas said grimacing. "I don't plan on doing anything that would land me on the business end of her weapon."

"Asking her to shut down the center might do the trick." Daron looked at him with a raised eyebrow.

In an obvious attempt to make the intense conversation light, "at least we know that my sister-in-law can handle a weapon," Jai replied. "She is a bad ass and that lets me know she'd be able to handle herself, when needed."

"There's no question that she can handle herself," Khalil added.

"The fact remains that I'm her husband," Vikkas said, "but it's my primary job to ensure her safety and security for the rest of our lives. Isn't that what you all have been doing with your significant others?"

Jai stiffened, under the weight of Vikkas' glare. "Of course, I get it, brother. Just trying to make you come to terms with the fact that your wife is an OG. A woman who commands respect and deserves it and might resent your interference."

When it came to the bronze beauty who had stolen his heart when they were teens, Vikkas would obliterate anyone or anything threatening her. He was happy that they were peacefully enjoying their married life, far away from their unstable relatives, but the looming trouble was going to disrupt that reality.

Things had calmed down after dealing with and distancing themselves from her drama filled family in the states that almost caused her to end up in an early grave. Par for the course since the Kings and Knights had a fair share of having to take drastic measures protecting the women in their lives. Granted, these beauties were more than capable of handling their business as evidenced by the fact that Daron's woman, Cameron, was a natural gunslinger. A trait that Vikkas didn't realize Milan had as well until someone forced her hand.

"Vikkas, are you still with us?" Jai asked, chuckling.

Focusing on his brother, he said, "You know you're a pain in the ass, right?"

"Oh geez, here we go," Jai taunted, but his humor was infectious. "Really, man?"

"Absolutely, but I wouldn't trade you for anyone else." He smiled. "I love you, man."

Giving him a playful nudge in the side, Jai replied, "Please stop with all of that, you're making me nauseous."

With the heat of his father's eyes on him, Vikkas threw up his hands and focused on the rest of his Castle family entering the room. He greeted his brothers. In the forefront of his mind, he knew the conversation with Khalil, Jai, and Daron wasn't over. These men were notorious for not letting go of a discussion until they were satisfied their points had been made and taken seriously.

After everyone greeted each other, they took their seats around a semi-circle conference table that was an exact replica of the one in the Castle back in the United States. The only person missing was Sheikh Kamran, but they'd been told by his personal security escort team that he was in route.

Taking in the power of the men sitting around the table and those on the dropdown screen, no doubt they'd be able to deal with whatever came their way. So much talent and unique skill sets wrapped up in all of these men. Whoever mustered up enough bravery to challenge them or those they loved had better be prepared for the wrath.

Fifteen minutes later, Sheikh Kamran greeted everyone in person as well as those attending virtually. The meeting was planned for about two hours so they could share the latest intel, discuss, and strategize on what steps they'd be taking to deal with the current threats. Vikkas turned his attention to the matters at hand. The quicker they made it through this meeting, the sooner he would be able to get home to his wife.

Chapter 3

Sipping a glass of Moscato, Milan relaxed and was now ready to embark on the new expansion. Standing, she closed her eyes and embraced the peacefulness surrounding her. Feeling his presence, she didn't turn around, but a smile etched its way onto her lips.

Large, muscular arms circled her waist, then a gentle kiss pressed on the soft curve of her neck. That one touch ignited a fiery sensation throughout Milan's body. Only one man had ever made her feel this way and she was now lucky enough to be married to him, a King in his own right. Prestigious, even without his Castle affiliation.

His cologne provided a pleasant scent that made her inhale the pure male essence of him. She was totally enamored by the six-foot-two-inch man holding her curvaceous frame securely in his arms as though he never wanted to let her go. He made her feel safe and unconditionally loved. A far cry from what she thought she'd ever feel with a man. Especially since her family's blueprint favored thugs and ex-cons.

"What are you thinking about, my love?" Vikkas whispered against her ear.

Eyes closed and inhaling the light, aquatic scent again, she said, "Hi baby, I missed you today."

"I missed you too beautiful, but that's not what I asked." He used his long, tapered fingers to angle her chin so she could look in his eyes and waited patiently for her response.

Turning completely in his arms, Milan gazed up into the dark brown depths of his eyes. "I was thinking about everything that will need to go into the upgrade process."

"There's nothing to worry about, my love," he said in a calm tone, but a little lift at the end of the words meant something was going on. "Everything is in order."

With all of the construction going on and new businesses springing up in Durabia, the paperwork and security measures had to be precise. The current opposition rising up against the sweeping reforms Kamran had implemented was increasing. No room for error was allowed due to the scrutiny of the Durabian count. Upheaval was already present because of the emerging interracial relationships and marriages - ones like Vikkas' and Milan's.

Sheikh Kamran and Sheikha Ellena had set off a firestorm when they united. As more interracial relationships emerged, the old guard were doing their best to intervene and stop this from becoming the norm to preserve Durabia's purity. However, that was hard to do when you have a number of transplant couples coming to live in your country.

After a few minutes of basking in a sensuous embrace, Milan placed a kiss on the fabric near his heart, refrained from questioning his tone, and said, "I know, just don't want anything to go wrong."

Vikkas gazed into her eyes, as if trying to read into her soul, then leaned down to place a comforting kiss on her lips that sent a tingle all the way to her toes.

"I'm going to take a shower, care to keep me company?" he asked in a mischievous tone and a slow lift of his eyebrows.

"Are you trying to distract me, husband?" Milan asked in what she hoped was a seductive tone.

"Well, why don't you join me and find out," he challenged, unbuttoning his shirt.

A smile spread across her face when she was amused. Yes, he was definitely trying to keep her mind off something. She replied, "I'll be there in a minute, let me get everything off the table."

"Don't take too long, I'll be waiting."

Watching as Vikkas swaggered away, Milan's gaze followed his every move. He was aware of her looking in his direction and gave a wink over his shoulder. After he was out of her line of sight, she gathered up her laptop, notebook and near empty glass of Moscato that she polished off in one drink. Excitement and anticipation filled her as she went to join her husband.

One hour later, after an erotic climax filled shower, Milan listened to the light sounds of pots and pans on the stove as Vikkas fixed them dinner. Even though she did a lot of the cooking, he had insisted on being the chef tonight. Evidently her bedroom skills had brought out the culinary skills in him.

Enjoying the smells of the Indian seasoned lamb, sweet rice, and mixed vegetables, she sat back relaxed on a plush cardinal red couch. Basking in the afterglow of their lovemaking, Milan leaned her head back on the pillows, she closed her eyes and slipped into a sated slumber.

Chapter 4

Soft kisses caressed her face causing Milan's eyelids to flutter open. Smiling as her gaze connected with Vikkas', she was immobilized by his intense stare. All she could do was remain silent, thank God that Khalil had sent him on a search for her while he was yet on the serious end of a lifesaving surgery. *"Go find your wife,"* Khalil had commanded. He did not mean the woman that Varsha had arranged for him to marry, despite Khalil's protest. He had meant Milan. After a few seconds, his baritone voice broke the silence.

"Are you hungry, my love?"

"Why didn't you wake me when you were done cooking?"

He shifted his stance. "You needed to rest, and the food is warming in the oven on a low setting. Besides, I enjoyed watching you sleep."

Placing her hand on his clean-shaven face, she whispered, "What can I say to that?"

"Let's go eat, woman. My stomach is already at the table waiting for us."

Raising an eyebrow, Milan welcomed the searing kiss he placed on her lips. Full of promise for more to come after they completed their meal. Her ravenous appetite needed to be quenched on both fronts. She'd never get enough of this man.

Over the rim of his glass, he asked, "Anything exciting happen today at work?"

Milan locked gazes with Vikkas suspecting that he already knew about the young man who unexpectedly appeared up at the center.

With all of the security in place, the Kings and Knights kept each other informed, especially when it came to their families.

"Is that a trick question?" she asked, her fork pausing in mid-air.

"Of course not, my love. It is a simple question, so why are you tap dancing around an answer?" he said in a calm tone, obviously trying to keep the conversation from getting contentious.

Milan had been avoiding an argument with him, feeling deep down information was being kept form her. His current question was getting under her skin because she knew that he prided himself on knowing everything that was happening. That was the *"King of the Castle"* way of operating.

Placing her utensil on the edge of the plate, she sighed, "Really, Vikkas. I'm sure you know everything that happens at the center."

He took two more bites of lamb, then placed his fork down. As much as she loved the protection provided by the Kings and Knights, it was also an Achilles heel. There›d always been this sense of freedom that she cherished; to make some decisions and move on her own accord ever since her mother kicked her out at age fifteen and directly resulted from Pearline's own self-hatred and jealousy towards her.

"Yes, I know about your new guest. I won't apologize for making sure you are safe at all costs," he replied, and a hard edge crept into his voice. "You do realize where we are living and where your business is located, right?"

Inhaling then releasing a slow deep breath, she bit back on a sarcastic response. "I know and understand. It doesn't mean that I have to be a fan of these *extra measures* being taken," Milan said. "It has been a little overwhelming with the increased security and politics."

Reaching across the table, he laced their hands. She relaxed as he held them silently for a few seconds. "Baby, I know everything going on is a lot right now. Making sure danger stays as far away from you as possible is one of my responsibilities as your man. Don't fault me for that," Vikkas said in a tone that spoke of his adoration. *"Loving you with everything in me is real. My passion for moving heaven and earth to keep you safe will never end."*

Briefly, Milan's thoughts flashed back to the challenges they faced during their friendship and becoming a couple. Varsha played a huge part in separating them because of her bias about interracial dating and the fact that Milan hailed form Englewood. A low-income neighborhood on the south side of Chicago, while Vikkas' family was her family's definition of filthy rich. Then she pushed her son towards an arranged marriage that his father didn't approve of. Then years later, the man showed up at her office. This time around she wasn't letting him go. As eventful as their wedding was, it served as the symbol of their unbroken bond and love.

Giving her hand a gentle squeeze, she looked at him feeling so much love for this man it hurt. "Honey, I get that and I'm not complaining. Sometimes it gets a little stifling. You mean the world to me. I love you for loving me the way that you do."

Her breathing hitched as she watched Vikkas push his chair away from the table. He walked around to gather her into his arms. Sweetly kissing her forehead, the couple stood quietly surrounded by the love transmitting from one to the other. Heading into the living room, minutes later, she laid her head on his muscular, comforting chest as they cuddled on the couch.

The spacious room they sat in was smaller in comparison to their Chicago suburban mansion. The 10,000 square foot, two-level house in Durabia was a mini replica of their 20,000 square foot home in the States. The earth tone and vibrant color schemes, decorations of abstract art and furniture throughout were similar because Milan wanted everything to make them feel at home. Vikkas made sure that her requests were all taken care of.

Chapter 5

An hour later, Vikkas glanced over at his wife sleeping peacefully on the couch. They'd been talking about the challenges he was having cleaning up the fallout with his family and then dozed off. After covering her up with the purple throw, he walked into the kitchen to clean up. Heavy thoughts swirled in his mind about everything going on, including the Kings and Knights putting countermeasures in place for the pending war and how that would affect her as well.

They were working strategically and in stealth mode, ready to handle the chaos but hoping the casualties could be kept at a minimum. A lot of enemies had been made, due to Kamran moving away from the traditional ways of operating in the Durabian kingdom. Those who had been banished to Nadaum had been plotting to overthrow the new implanted Sheikh's reign. Kamran, Ellena, and their children were in danger again.

Peering into the living room, Vikkas checked on his wife who was still sleeping soundly. He headed into his office to make a phone call. Whenever he was feeling unsettled, talking to the person who always gave him wise counsel was calming.

"Hello, my son, is everything all right?" Khalil asked.

"Hello, father," he replied settling into his office chair. "Did I disturb you?"

"Hold on for a moment, Vikkas," he said.

Hearing a muffled conversation between his father and mother, he realized they must have been getting ready to retire for the night. A minute later, he heard footsteps echoed on the other end signaling his father was on the move. If he had to guess, the elder Germaine was heading to his home office for some privacy. Not that he didn't share important things with his wife, but Khalil definitely filtered the information after he'd decided on what was necessary to share and what needed to be taken to the grave.

"Son, I'm here. What is wrong?" Khalil responded, concern lacing his voice.

"Nothing's wrong," he replied, then thought better of holding that stance. "I've been a little concerned about all of planning and increased security measures we've been working on."

"Is your wife upset by everything we are doing? At least the parts that she knows?"

Always amazed with his father's perceptive nature, Vikkas chuckled. "Hmm, what made you come to that conclusion?"

"You forget I know both of you very well. Milan is a beautiful soul, who doesn't take too kindly to feeling controlled," Khalil responded. "We both know she loves her independence and taking the lead. You have to respect that and still find a way to protect her without making her feel you believe she's a damsel in distress."

Sighing loudly, Vikkas said, "You're absolutely right, father. But she can't control this situation. There's too many dangerous people involved in this scenario."

"How much information have you shared with her?"

"What I can share based on our Castle code, father. You know how I feel about keeping secrets from her, but I made a pact and honoring that is equally important," Vikkas said. "The balance is a struggle for me right now because I love that woman and don't want to lose her trust. If she finds out we've been investigating the staff and residents behind her back and installed extra cameras without her knowledge, that trust will take a hit."

Vikkas waited while his father took a pause before responding, "Yes, son, I know. Believe me the martial bond is important, just as the brotherhood you entered into. If you need some couple's counseling, Aashna will also be there for you and Milan."

"I think we'll be fine, but I'll keep you on speed dial, just in case," he said. They talked a little more about the Maharaj family drama and then bid each other good night.

Vikkas leaned back in his office chair, confident in the support that he knew they'd have through all of this. His main concern was the fact that he couldn't speak openly about everything with his wife. Praying that a rift wouldn't form between them.

He clicked off the desk light and headed back to the living room. Besides the immediate concern, something was bothering his spirit. He had watched the video surveillance of that boy several times. Something was off. He couldn›t put his finger on it. Right now, he›d focus on the things within his current reach.

Tonight, he would enjoy the peacefulness surrounding them by turning his mind off of the things that they'd be facing when the sun rose tomorrow. Gathering Milan from the couch and cradling her in his arms, he carried her into the master bedroom. After placing her under the covers, he doubled-checked the security system then climbed into bed. His unspoken prayers were that they made it through this test. Pulling Milan to the center of the king-sized bed, Vikkas wrapped his body around hers and fell into a deep sleep.

Chapter 6

Across the Atlantic Ocean, heavy rainfall saturated the ground while thunder roared and created a deafening sound. In the distance, specks of lightning brightened the dark grey sky.

Two men sat at a round, mahogany table etched with gold accents in a dimly lit office. They scanned the furniture and zoned in on the expensive painting hanging on the wall. It depicted a three-dimensional, panoramic view of the Durabian skyline.

Fifteen minutes earlier, the two shady characters had been escorted into the house. One six-foot burly man kept them company while they awaited their host. One of them had revenge on his brain, while the other was along for the pay day connected to whatever it took to exact said revenge.

Once they agreed to the terms of this deal, there'd be no coming back from any associated consequences. Money was all that mattered. Everything else would be collateral damage.

"Gentlemen, I'm sorry to have kept you waiting," an elegant woman said, giving them a smile. She'd purposely made sure to take her time. Hidden cameras were strategically installed in the office, so she had been watching them the entire time.

Seth and Marcus gave her head nods then glanced at each other, but neither immediately spoke. The beauty approaching them was not a reflection of the darkness that resided within her soul. Standing five-feet-four inches tall with fair skin and long black silky hair hanging down her back, she walked with the confidence of a vixen.

"Welcome, gentlemen," she said in a sultry manner that made them sit up and take notice. "Are you ready to get down to business?"

"Can we at least get a drink before talking?" Seth asked.

"Of course, I apologize that Carlos wasn't more hospitable to you." With a slight smile, she sauntered over to the bar area. Usually, one of her staff would be fixing drinks but she didn't want anyone else to witness this meeting. *The less folks in the know, the better.*

"What's your poison?" she asked.

Seth requested a rum and coke but kept watching her cautiously. Evidently, he believed that she would be bold enough to add something suspicious to their drink. Marcus remained quiet.

Only one thing was on Varsha's mind. The consistent replay of the wedding reception from hell remained in the forefront of her mind. Embarrassment and feeling disrespected were still fresh for her. Not to mention the foiled attempt on Khalil's life.

Disdain filled her damaged soul thinking about Vikkas being married to Milan, despite everything she had done to prevent it from happening. She'd chosen to fade into the background, figuring out what the next move would be. Her family had banished her to Bahrain while the police were still searching for her. No extradition treaties to worry about and she was able to move around without fearing jail time. Luckily, Varsha found someone who wanted to cause suffering to the couple just as much as she did.

"So, are you ready to talk now?" Varsha asked, handing Seth his drink. She took a seat in the executive chair behind her desk. She didn't care that this would hurt the man that she raised from a young age and loved in her own way. The only way to hurt Khalil was through their son and the woman he had been secretly married to all these years. They did have an "edge", but she had the money and means.

After taking a gulp, Seth spoke up. "What's the next move?"

Varsha gave the man an appraising look, wanting to tell him what she really thought of him. That he was classless, ignorant, and gullible. One thing her mother taught was to mentally be a few steps ahead. No doubt that she was more cunning than these two individuals sitting across from her.

"Does that mean you are in?" she asked for clarity, taking a sip of her extra dry martini. Even though seething internally, Varsha was a great poker player. No one could detect the rage she felt at how her life had been one big lie. Though she had forced her family to dismantle Khalil's marriage to Aashna so she could have him for herself, he had been smart enough to find a loophole in the process that didn't come to light until Vikkas' marriage to Milan. He had played her and the entire family of fools, an even managed to stay legally married to the love of his life in order to protect her.

Sitting up straight, forward, and keeping an eye on the bodyguard nearby, Seth said, "Absolutely, but I have a few demands of my own."

Tapping her polished red nails on the desk, Varsha chuckled. "Of course, you do. I would be surprised if that wasn't the case. You people always want something." A chill swept through the room when those words escaped her lips.

"Who the hell is you people?" he snapped in an edgy tone, causing her bodyguard to take a half step forward.

She held up her right hand to stop the burly man's progress. Varsha wasn't afraid of Seth or his foolishness. As far as she was concerned, he was the means to an end. Anger and resentment drove him, so she'd play him as smoothly as a stringed instrument.

"I did not mean to offend you. My apologies," she replied in a smooth tone. "That statement was not meant to be personal."

Looking through her peripheral at the bodyguard, she caught him smirking. He wasn't fooled by her stellar acting skills. Varsha needed to hurry this meeting along, so she could relax with a hot bath and glass of Cabernet for the evening.

As the tension in the room diminished, a master plan was set, and no one would see them coming.

Chapter 7

Climbing the spiral staircase, after her two guests were gone, Varsha went upstairs to her massive bedroom suite. Decorated in red and gold, two of her favorite colors, the space served as her sanctuary. On the enclosed balcony, she settled on the custom-made wicker couch, breathing in the fresh air from the aftermath of the rainfall.

She took a little time to get her thoughts together before making a call. Her reach was far, thanks to her financial supporters, and the mole that she had planted in a critical office in Durabia. Actions had already been put into motion, even before Seth agreed to joining.

Varsha's secret travels overseas resulted in connecting with the current benefactors. She'd been contacted and made a visit to learn what common ground they all shared. Settling old scores and celebrating the demise of those who had wronged them. Made for the best of friends; didn't take more than that, along with the money, to get her onboard.

Thirty minutes later, she dialed a third number that was programmed in the burner phone. Several rings later the call was answered.

"What took you so long to answer the phone?" she snapped.

"I had to excuse myself and find a private place to talk. Or would you rather that I had this conversation in front of your son?"

After pausing for a brief moment, Varsha said, "I think you know better than to do that. After all, we are in this together."

"Exactly. You may want to keep that in mind when you are speaking to me since I'm doing your dirty work," he said in an overconfident manner.

"And you might want to remember who is funding this trip that you are on," she countered. No way she would allow him to talk to her this way. He was working for her.

The man was a smart individual and had proven to be resourceful. While she wouldn't provoke him because he had the potential to be a loose cannon, Varsha would not welcome any type of disrespect from someone in her pocket. She took a deep breath and remained silent for a few seconds to let him absorb the full weight of her words.

"My apologies, I didn't mean to offend you. It's been a tiresome day," his tone changed into a milder one. "There's still a lot to be done here. I'm trying to stay focused and not bring unnecessary attention to myself."

"Understood. We have much to do in a short period of time. Nothing can go wrong, so get some rest and make sure to check in with me as scheduled."

"I will, have a good night." A dial tone echoed into her ear. Varsha was not happy that he'd disconnected without her making sure their call was concluded.

Biding her time, she'd deal with him in person. Much sooner than he anticipated. Switching off and placing the burner phone in the nightstand drawer, she went into the bathroom to take a shower. While removing her makeup, a sly smile lifted on her lips.

She was envisioning victory without the help of her family members. Men who thought they had everything figured out and were in control but failed each time. Khalil Germaine had proven that to be the case. Vengeance would be enjoyable for her. No one would be spared - Khalil, Vikkas, Jaidev, and most important Milan. They would all pay.

Chapter 8

Sunshine peered through the window awakening Milan. Vikkas had partially opened their motorized blackout shades as he loved watching the sunrise and was up right before dawn. That man could get three hours of sleep and still manage as if he rested for a full eight hours.

Reaching over to his side of the bed, she grabbed the remote from the nightstand and brought the room back to a complete darkness. As soon as she placed her head back on the pillow to get a little more shuteye, the bedroom door opened. She cracked one eye slightly enough to find Vikkas walking towards the bed with a breakfast tray.

"Baby, why is it so dark in here?"

"You know why genius," she teased.

He settled the tray on the nightstand, dropped down on the bed and kissed her forehead.

"Don't try to soften me up," she scoffed. "I love you, but I'm not liking you right now."

Smirking and shaking his head, his dark brown eyes pierced hers. "My love, you need to eat. It'll be time for us to head to the center soon."

"Um, what do you mean by we?"

"We're going to the center together today. Now, eat and get yourself together woman." Without blinking, he didn't back down from his statement. "I'll be down in the office. Love you."

With that, her husband walked out of the room. As much as he could be bossy and a little domineering, she could match him on both fronts. Sitting up, she settled the tray on her lap and enjoyed the vegetable omelet, ambrosia, and freshly squeezed orange juice.

Soon after, Milan showered, dressed in a ruffled white blouse, dark jeans, and three-inch black ankle boots. Feeling refreshed and ready for the day, she headed downstairs still wondering about his sudden interest in going to her office today.

"Are you ready to go, my love?" he asked, without looking up from the document he held. Even though her husband had his head buried in legal correspondence, Vikkas was well aware of her presence.

"I left kindergarten years ago. You know I can go to the center by myself, right?"

"I know that you are perfectly capable of doing so. However, today, I'll be tagging along," Vikkas said in a matter-of-fact tone that did not have her fooled in the least.

Folding her arms underneath her ample bosom, she asked, "Why? Is there something going on that I don't know about, again?"

Threats against the center was the main point of contention in their marriage. Information that the Kings and Knights received were not being talked about with their Queens. Milan made her unhappiness about this known to him on several occasions.

He stood and walked over to her, a calculated move to distract her. Looking deeply in her eyes, he planted a kiss on her lips with no further response.

Thirty minutes later, they parked in one of the reserved spaces at the center. Milan glanced over, placing a hand on Vikkas› arm. She hadn't spoken a word since they left the house. The frustration about everything happening, plus feeling as if he was keeping things from her were taking a toll.

This man would move heaven and earth for her. No doubt about that. But she didn't do well with secrets, especially from those closest to her.

"I love you honey. Thank you for coming in with me today," she said shaking off the inner turmoil.

"And I love you too baby." He lifted her hand to his mouth, sweetly kissed it. "Lead the way, so we don't have to be here all day. We have other things to do."

"Really now? What would that be?"

"I might have a few surprises up my sleeve," he replied, kissed her before sliding out of the car.

Milan smiled, watching him walk around the car to open her door. If she had attempted to get out, it would have sparked an attitude. He was not only fiercely protective, but a true gentleman. A far cry from the type of man her mother wanted for her life. Pearline had been loyal to a man serving a sentence. Well as loyal as her body allowed her to be. She certainly gave the appearance of being alone, but her daughters had to witness those late-night appearances and early morning exits from men she found would take what they wanted without asking for money.

Hand in hand, they walked into the center being greeted by members of the staff.

Sitting down in the leather executive chair behind her desk, Milan turned on her computer and checked emails while Vikkas took a phone call from his brother Jai. Glancing up at her husband, she smiled. Even when they had their disagreements, they still managed to work through it.

Getting back to the task at hand, her mind refocused on the messages that she'd been checking. One immediately caught her attention. The subject line read, *"Your Days Are Numbered"* while the short email gave a brief warning that there would be an attack on the center.

Milan gasped which caught the attention of Vikkas who walked up behind her and peered at the screen. "Who sent this?" he asked with a hint of anger in his voice.

She looked up at him. "I don't know, baby."

She already knew what would happen next. He sent a quick text and his infamous game face fell into place. Tempted to ask questions, she decided against it. They would wait until they left the center.

"Are you ready to go meet and talk to my newest resident, Jonathan?" she asked. After the email, Milan knew that Vikkas was not letting her out of his sight.

"Lead the way, my love," he said. Milan pushed away from the desk, stood and they headed to the hub of the center.

Chapter 9

Entering into the center's common area, Milan and Vikkas made immediate eye contact with Jonathan. Today he seemed more relaxed and at home unlike the panicked way he had when he first arrived, then the guarded look that followed when she tried to question him.

Milan smiled, casually crossing one leg over the other as she sat across from him. Her husband had an impartial look on his face. Always assessing and observing a person's body language.

"How did you sleep last night Jonathan?" she asked.

"Good, thank you," he replied then lowered his gaze to the linoleum floor.

Sensing his slight discomfort, she gestured to her right. "Jonathan, this is my husband, Vikkas Germaine."

"It's nice to meet you."

Jonathan received a simple nod from Vikkas and she wanted to chide him for being so openly distrustful.

After a few more minutes of light conversation, Milan eased her way into the harder part of the exchange.

Jonathan shared that he was from Dashma, a small city in Nadaum. Chills ran down Milan's spine, though she appeared unfazed by his revelation. A number of teens were running from that place for a variety of reasons. Escaping from the dictatorship, kidnapping of youth, and poverty-stricken cities. In turn, they were looking for a chance to live a different type of life and experience their desired freedom. .

"So, Jonathan, how did you hear about my wife's center?" Vikkas asked. Surprising everyone because he'd been quiet during the exchange between Milan and Jonathan, mentally taking notes.

"Word of this place has been spreading fast," he replied. "Due to the trouble, we've been facing and looking for an escape from it. That's the reason I made the journey here," he said.

"Well, that's quite admirable. I'm sure it was also scary as well," Milan interjected when Vikkas did not respond.

"I can't fight for something I don't believe in."

At that moment, Vikkas' cell rang and he glanced at the screen. "Please excuse me, I have to take this call. I'll be back shortly."

Milan's gaze briefly met his, but she didn't react.

Her attention focused back on Jonathan. She asked him about his family but received vague answers. Milan felt as if they were playing a game of cat and mouse.

Mastering psychology and using it to her advantage is what she did to gain insight into people. Intelligence, street smarts, and discernment was part of her DNA. Not too much got past her, so she could be patient while trying to get him to open up.

"Jonathan, would you like to take a walk?"

He glanced in the direction where Vikkas disappeared. "Shouldn't we wait for your husband?"

"No, he'll catch up with us," Milan said with what she hoped was a reassuring smile.

A strange look crossed Jonathan's face, but he tried to mask it. Milan didn't comment on it, figuring he thought she hadn't witnessed the change. They went past the front desk, dining area, and weight room to the indoor walking track.

Maybe they could get one or two laps in before Vikkas rejoined them. It'd give her an opportunity to encourage the evasive young man to relax a little. She kept wondering why Vikkas was acting so strange.

As they began conversing about simple things such as his favorite foods and sports, the tension seemed to lift a little. Three other people were in the area, one young man running with earbuds on while two young ladies were taking a leisurely stroll and having an animated conversation about their latest crush.

Glancing over his shoulder from time to time, Jonathan was expecting see Vikkas show up. Noticing his less than subtle movements, Milan kept the conversation and mild pace around the track.

"How are you enjoying this walk?" she asked, drawing his full attention back to her.

He gave her a grin. "This is nice. The center is much bigger than it looks from the outside."

"Yes, it is. We try to offer as much as we can here to make life as normal as possible for our guests."

"I've never seen anything like this in my life," he exclaimed sweeping a gaze at the girls as they walked past. "It's really amazing."

"So, Jonathan, what are your plans? Is there something you're passionate about doing?"

Observing his thought-provoking reaction to her question, she could tell that he hadn't really been thinking that far ahead. His silence also fueled that theory. This question seemed to stump the new ones every time. Because they were running away from something, it never dawned on them to run to something positive.

"It's important that you do, Jonathan. As I've learned over the years, your life and motivation are dependent upon where you see yourself. Your goals and aspirations, it makes things clear."

Sensing his unease, she said, "You don't have to have an answer today, it's important to think about what you'd like your future to reflect."

"That makes sense. I never thought about it because my survival has been day to day," he answered. "Thank you. I haven't anyone to ask me that before, so I focus on my destiny."

Glancing at the platinum watch on her left wrist, Milan silently wondered where Vikkas could be since he was suspicious of Jonathan, and she still had no clear reason why.

Chapter 10

In a hidden corner of the track, Vikkas watched as his wife and Jonathan took laps around the indoor track. Finishing his call, he headed straight to the area but decided to wait for a few minutes before approaching them. Something didn't feel right about this young man. In the video his movements and actions seemed contrived as though they had been rehearsed.

Sending Milan into a panic was not what Vikkas intended to do. However, new concerns had risen among the Kings and Knights. Information that he still couldn't share with her right now. They'd already been at odds because he was being super vague about everything going on behind the scenes. An unfortunate position to be in with the woman you vowed to honest with and open to for the rest of your lives.

Everyone was put on a high alert. The latest intel had prompted that phone call from his father a few moments ago. The Kings, Knights, and their spouses were being called to attend a meeting at the palace.

Milan and Jonathan were still engaged in a lively conversation, and it made his heart happy that his beautiful spouse was able to do what she loved. Transforming lives was one of her greatest passions. He was angered that someone was trying to sabotage that, bringing harm to her and the center itself.

Finally moving past the commercial water dispensers, lockers and catching up with them, he laced one of his wife's hands in his, asking, "Did you miss me?"

"Of course, I missed you," Milan responded with a twinkle of mischief in her eyes.

He was amused at the side eye Jonathan gave him. Quick, but not subtle. In the meantime, he planted a gentle kiss on her lips.

"How many laps have you done?" he asked, falling into their stride.

Laughing, Milan said, "I don't even know because we were talking."

"We've done about ten laps," Jonathan shared.

"Wow, I'm glad that you were paying attention," she said smiling, and he returned one to her.

The trio finished the current lap, then headed back to the common area of the center. The ease of conversation had shifted in the silence that ensued. Jonathan's guard was back up, which didn't go unnoticed. Milan indicated that she and Vikkas were leaving and for a moment paused to see how he reacted.

After touching base with the staff and security, the couple made their way to their custom-built Black Onyx Lexus LX570. Momentary silence filled the luxury SUV until they merged onto the highway.

Breaking the quietness, Milan asked, "Vikkas, why were you trying to intimidate that young man?"

"Baby, what are you talking about?" he asked, trying, but failing to sound innocent.

This time she was the one to give him a side eye. "You know *exactly* what I'm talking about."

"You can stop with the sassiness, my love. If Jonathan was frightened, then he could've fooled me. I guess you didn't notice the attitude shift when I interrupted your stroll."

Laughing, she shook her head. "What are you talking about? I'm going to need you to be a little more specific."

Glancing over at Vikkas, she asked, "Honey, are you jealous?"

"Jealous of who? That kid? I don't think so. You do realize that I'm a grown ass man, right?"

"Well, you could've fooled me since you seem to be a little bothered."

Smirking, while still keeping his eyes on the road, Vikkas simply replied, "I have receipts. I could remind you of how grown I am. You do remember last night and this morning, right?"

He knew that his slick comeback caught his very vocal wife off guard. Because the couple were so in tune with each other, Vikkas knew exactly why that smile lifted the corners of her mouth.

"Of course I know that," she said. "But it sounds like you feel the need to remind me."

Taking a quick glance at her then putting his focus back on the road, he replied, "As soon as we're done with the group meeting, then I will gladly do that and more."

As smoothly as he had said it, Vikkas meant that with every fiber of his being. He tapped his fingers on the steering wheel, humming the hook to Marvin Gaye's classic song, "Let's Get It On."

In his peripheral vision, he found Milan holding in a laugh because he couldn't carry a tune if it came with handles. He'd temporarily shut down the conversation about Jonathan, but knew she'd bring it back up when they got home. Right now, he wanted to keep their interaction lighthearted.

"All right, you win this round. Know this conversation isn't over, Mr. Germaine. And, for the record, I think you need to be reminded of how grown your woman is."

Reaching for the hand in her lap, while he navigated through the building traffic on the highway, he said, "No worries, my love. I already know the treasure that I have in my life. It's going to be a fun night when we get home."

Bringing Milan's hand to his lips, he kissed it then gently placed it back down. His focus shifted to their current destination to meet up with the Kings, Knights, and Queens. He was surprised that Khalil had called everyone in on such short notice.

Chapter 11

After clearing security at the front gate of the Durabian palace, Vikkas drove one mile under the marble archway to Sheikh Kamran and Sheikha Ellena's primary residence. He passed several rows of palm trees planted on each side of the driveway and a three-tier stone fountain surrounded by a sea of red and yellow flowers. The exterior of the palace had gold trimmings and dome shaped ceilings created to capture attention.

"I love this. It's always breathtaking to see," Milan said as their car pulled up to the front of the palace.

"I agree. It is a beautiful sight," Vikkas smiled while looking at his wife.

Glancing over to find where his focus had landed, she returned his smile and blushed. He was elated to be the man who received those reactions out of her daily.

A line of familiar vehicles was ahead of them, so Vikkas parked, and they walked towards one of the exterior corridors.

Standing outside, near the meeting room entrance, Khalil was finishing a phone call. Dressed in black slacks with a long sleeve silk shirt, he smiled as Vikkas and Milan approached followed by two palace security guards. This was the most casual of garments she'd ever seen on him.

"Hello, Father."

"Good evening, Son." This man was the spitting image of Vikkas, who had always been his right hand as Khalil completed a five-year spiritual tour.

Vikkas stepped aside so his father could greet and embrace Milan. "Welcome, Daughter." Khalil never shied away from embraces to those he loved dearly, despite the traditional customs in Durabia about public affection.

"Hi, Khalil," Milan welcomed his embrace, and then asked, "Are we the last two to arrive?"

"No, we are still waiting on Sheikh Kamran and Sheikha Ellena to arrive. They were called away, but should be here shortly," Khalil shared. "In the meantime, we are having some light cocktails and appetizers. Cameron, Aashna, and Temple are inside if you'd like to join them."

Glancing between both men and smirking, Milan said, "just say that you need to talk to Vikkas. Love you both."

Vikkas watched his wife walk through and disappear inside the exterior meeting room doors. Shaking his head, he looked at Khalil, "that's your feisty daughter-in-law."

"Yes, I love her and you two together."

"Father, why are you out here on the phone? Did something else happen?"

"Always so perceptive, much like your siblings. The three of you don't miss much of anything," he chuckled thinking about the traits that each of his children shared with him.

"You can thank your DNA for that," Vikkas said.

Turning the conversation to a more serious tone, Khalil looked over his shoulder to make sure no one else was within earshot. Vikkas listened as his father told him about the latest intel the Kings had received. The Nadaum cell had increased their recruiting mission and concerns were that some of their loyal followers were in Durabia.

High level background checks were being done on newly hired staff at the palace and youth at the center. The planned attack against Durabia leadership, the Kings, and anyone associated with them was imminent.

"Sheikh Kamran and I want to talk to everyone," Khalil said. "We are including our Queens at this meeting because it's important for them to know some of the information that we can share right now."

"I'm glad to hear that we can share some things. Milan hasn't been too happy with me," Vikkas shared, feeling apprehensive because he would still have to keep secrets from his wife." There's been a little tension developing between us."

"Son, I understand and feel your pain. Aashna isn't aware of everything. Cameron is the only exception to the Kings rule."

"Pray for me because you already know Milan likes to be well informed. That woman should have worked for the CIA, FBI or Secret Service."

Laughing to lighten the mood, both men shook their heads and exhaled a deep breath. Vikkas and Khalil tracked the progress of one of the royal security team members rounding the corner of the palace. He came to let them know the royal couple were on their way.

"We'd better head in and join everyone," Vikkas said. "Besides, I need to lay eyes on my wife."

"Yes, I know that you can't stay away from Milan too long. That woman has had your nose wide open for years now."

"Whatever do you mean?" he laughed, trying to imitate a British speaking voice but failing miserably.

"Let's go, Son. I feel the need to check on my wife too."

"You don't say, old wise man. I guess I'm not the only one who has been sprung."

Sharing one final glance, the two went inside to see their wives and join in on some of the conversations. Walking over to his wife, Vikkas leaned down kissing her on the cheek. Wrapping his arm around her waist, he greeted Daron and Cameron who were having an animated chat with Milan.

"Did you have a nice chat with your father?" she chuckled.

"You're not funny, sweetheart," Vikkas shared a fake scowl at her.

"Come on, man, I know it couldn't have been that bad," Daron chimed in.

"Next time, I'll make sure that you are included. Then we'll see if you'll be saying that."

Glancing over her shoulder, Milan said, "I'm sure you're being a drama king. Khalil is an angel."

Vikkas cast a penetrating look at his wife, thinking to himself *"I'm going to show you how much of a drama king I can be later on."*

Clearing their throats, Daron and Cameron looked at Vikkas and Milan then shook their heads. He glanced innocently at them and said, "don't hate. I know how you two roll." They all began chuckling lightly, then watched as Khalil and Aashna walked over to them. Daron and Cameron excused themselves to go over and grab something to drink.

Conversations halted and everyone's attention turned to the entrance of Sheikh Kamran and Sheikha Ellena. The meeting had unexpectedly been delayed by twenty minutes. Vikkas and Milan had been talking to Khalil and his wife Aashna. Planned dinners, future vacations and grandchildren were discussed.

The latter subject had the couple speechless and caught off guard. Children were in their future; however, they weren't rushing into parenthood just yet. It was a relief for them when the royal highnesses walked in, putting a halt to the current verbal exchange.

"Apologies for us being a little late to the party, we had to check in with one of our children," he said, while shaking his head. "These periodic meltdowns are something for the record books."

Milan, along with some of the other ladies, snickered as the Sheikha Ellena looked over at her husband and rolled her eyes. Even though the couple were royalty and ruled an entire country, they were down to earth people. High respect was given to them because of their humbleness.

"Hello everyone," Sheikha Ellena said. "As my husband shared, we apologize for being a little late. Never a dull moment when you have to get one of your children in check."

Sheikh Kamran slightly coughed, then asked everyone in the room to take a seat. He knew better than to comment any further.

"I hope their child is still breathing," Milan whispered to Vikkas.

"Me and you both," he laughed.

Everyone got settled in their seats around the large, gold accented mahogany conference table. At the same time, the projection screen was queued for those members who needed to conference in virtually. Once all of that was complete, they turned their attention to Sheikh Kamran and Khalil who were seated near one another at one end.

Roughly two hours later, goodbyes were shared as the Castle members began their departures from the palace. Sheikh Kamran, Khalil and Vikkas were still talking while Sheikha Ellena and Milan engaged in a private conversation. Jai and Temple had taken Aashna home because she knew her husband would still be a while wrapping things up at the palace.

"Milan, how have you been?" Sheikh Ellena asked. "It's been a while since we've seen each other due to our crazy schedules."

"I know, I've missed our gatherings especially with just the ladies getting together."

"Trust me, I really need one of those outings. You know I love my husband, but sometimes a break is needed from him and our children."

"Granted, Vikkas and I don't have children yet, but I do need a break from him," Milan chimed in. "I love that man. However, I'm in need of some girl time."

"Unfortunately, it might be a while before we are able to do that. Kamran's family is a piece of work. I knew that they were waiting to stir up mess, but this is on a whole other level of crazy."

Sighing and shaking her head, Milan's frustration was evident. "As bad as this may sound, I wonder what people would do if a firing squad was implemented. Would they rethink their actions?"

"Well, Annie Oakley, I don't know that they would really care," Sheikh Ellena laughed. "It seems as if they are on a suicide mission because they don't like the changes happening in this country."

While waiting on their husbands, they decided to stand outside and enjoy the nice, evening weather. Palace guards flanked them but kept a respectable distance to give them privacy. After stopping at the gold accented banister, Milan was the first to continue speaking.

"Ellena, I love living in Durabia. It has been a blessing, allowing me to make a difference. For someone or some people to use the disadvantaged youth as a pawn, it's disturbing."

Sighing, she responded, "I agree. But we know they won't get away with any of the things that are planned."

"We are a formidable family, aren't we?" Milan said.

"Yes, indeed. I am grateful that we all have each other's backs. That's rare and means a lot, especially with everything that we are facing."

"One thing is for sure, whoever is coming for us better make sure that they are ready for this smoke."

"Oh Lord, there you go again," Sheikha Ellena said.

Both women began laughing hysterically. As serious as the matter was, they needed this moment of comic relief. Despite their Castle family being primary targets, courtesy of the vengeance filled residents of Nadaum, all of it members were prepared to do battle.

Their main goal was to flush out the leaders of this misguided plot. Once those individuals were front and center, then the Kings, Knights and Queens would make sure a clear message was sent to anyone who thought their methods could outmatch those of the Castle and Durabian Palace.

Looking back towards the conference room, Milan said, "I think we'd better go break up the party involving our men. They've had enough time to talk and strategize."

Nodding in agreement, Sheikha Ellena looped her arm through Milan's and they headed back indoors. At a safe distance, the guards followed the women back to the conference room. Vikkas, Khalil, and Sheikha Kamran looked over as everyone entered back through the glass doors.

Smiling, Milan walked over and stood by her husband. "Okay, gentleman, I think it's time to wrap this up. We've been here a while and I know we'll be seeing each other again soon."

"Yes, dear," Vikkas replied with a mischievous twinkle in his eyes. "I almost forgot there are a few things that we need to take care of after we drop Father off at home."

"Are there now?" she asked innocently, not batting an eye.

Sheikh Kamran and Khalil cleared their throats. Everyone caught on to the innuendo that was shared between the couple. Sheikha Ellena seductively looked at her husband and that was all it took for him to say goodnight.

Chapter 13

Lively conversation between Milan and Khalil about the young people at her center and the progress being made sounded throughout the Lexus SUV, as light jazz played in the background. Vikkas was driving them to his father's house since Khalil had stayed back after the palace meeting to talk with Sheikh Kamran about some additional logistics that they didn't want to discuss in front of the entire group.

"Milan, I'm very proud of the work that you've been doing with the youth," Khalil began. "You know that one of the Castle's primary functions is helping to foster positive change in the lives of others."

"Yes, I do. It's one of the many reasons that I respect what you've built so much," she said.

"Things have evolved over the years because of the efforts by the Kings, Knights and now Queens. How would you feel about becoming an official member of the Castle?" Khalil asked.

Glancing over at Vikkas then looking in the rearview mirror, Milan asked, "what exactly does that mean?"

"It means that you have been invited to become a full member of the Castle. There are a lot of privileges that come with this assignment," he replied. "I will let my son talk to you some more about it and then we'll revisit this conversation. Is that okay?"

"Yes, I'm fine with that. Thank you, Khalil," she said.

Ten minutes before reaching their destination, Khalil made a quick call to Aashna to let her know that he would be arriving home soon. His voice lowered when he responded to something his wife said during their conversation. Vikkas and Milan glanced at each other and smiled.

"Smooth talker, aren't you father?" Vikkas arched an eyebrow while glancing at Khalil in the rear-view mirror.

"You really should mind your own business, son."

Milan released the laughter that she'd been holding in.

Right before Khalil exited the car, he looked at them both and said, "when you get home get started on a grandchild for me. That should keep you busy and not focused on me. "

"What is wrong with you, Father?" Vikkas laughed even though he was silently counting down the seconds until Khalil got out of the car. He was ready to get Milan home and handle their business. He made a promise to her earlier that he intended on keeping.

"Make me proud, son. I'm praying for twins," Khalil shared.

"And who is going to carry and give birth to these twins, Khalil?" Milan asked, trying her best to sound shocked.

"You got this. Love you both," Khalil said.

"Goodnight, Father."

"Goodnight, Khalil. Love you back," Milan replied.

Vikkas glanced over at his wife after his father entered the house. That man didn't have a filter. Khalil spoke his mind unapologetically and influenced them to do the same.

"Is there something that you need, Vikkas ?" Milan asked seductively.

"I'm going to show you exactly what I need in a few minutes." He switched the music to Teddy Pendergrass' song "Close the Door."

"Bring it, King of Wilmette," she said, with a raised eyebrow.

"I will and much more, my love. Let's go home." He reached their home in twenty minutes. As soon as the car was inside the garage and the door lowered, Vikkas shut off the engine and turned in Milan's direction. Unbuckling her seatbelt, he ran his index finger in a slow manner over her parted lips and stopped its descent in the cleft of her breasts. Locking eyes with her for a few seconds, Vikkas exited the car and walked over to open her door. As soon as the passenger door was shut, he pulled her into a passionate kiss.

Vikkas had Milan's naked body wrapped securely and held firmly against his sculpted frame. Allowing his heart rate to slow down, it was still a blur how they made it into the bedroom.

The talk about children and all that was going on around them got him to thinking about their present life.

"What's on your mind?" the sweet sound of Milan's voice brought him out of his thoughts.

"Just thinking about us and what it would be like to start on our family now rather than later," he responded honestly.

"When we talked about this the decision was made to wait a couple of years," she said. "What has changed?"

"My love, I'm not trying to pressure you. Plans do change."

Complete silence filled the room. He could hear his wife breathing lightly. Vikkas thought she'd fallen asleep.

"Let's get through all of this stuff we're dealing with. After that, then I promise we can revisit this conversation. Is that okay?"

"Close your eyes and sleep, my love." Milan didn't miss the fact that he hadn't answered her question.

Yawning, she said, "okay, I will in a minute. First, tell me about these privileges that come with Castle membership."

"I was wondering when you would bring that back up," he chuckled, while dodging her sharp elbow.

"My love, it means that I wouldn't have to keep so many secrets from you. You would be sitting at the table hearing mostly everything from the onset," Vikkas shared.

"I thought once we were married, that wouldn't be an issue," Milan said.

"It doesn't work that way, sweetheart. Marriage doesn't automatically make you a member. Father doesn't give out these invitations on a whim."

Taking a deep breath, Milan looked into his eyes. "I understand. So, now I have to make the decision about whether or not to become a Queen of the Castle."

"Yes, but you don't have to do that tonight. Sleep, my love."

He adjusted his body, so that his wife could get more comfortable. While she fell asleep, Vikkas' racing thoughts kept him up for another hour. So much to consider and get done. One thing he was sure of is that no matter what was decided, they were in this for the long haul.

Chapter 14

Placing the telephone in its holder, Vikkas finished adding notes to the electronic file of a new client. He encouraged his paralegal and executive assistant to leave a little early because they'd been working long hours. Due to an increase in new businesses launching in the area and his international law expertise, Vikkas' clientele base was growing.

Looking up at the clock and then the desk photo of his wife, he knew it was time to shut down for the day. However, he had one call to make before leaving the office. The Kings, Knights, along with a few of the Queens were working around the clock to implementing safety measures. They were on a mission to help the country evolve in regard to race relations and technology.

Vikkas picked up the phone and dialed.

"What's up brother?" Daron answered.

"Hey D, what's going on man?"

Laughing, Daron said, "You really need to stop trying to sound hip with your proper self."

"Whatever man. Don't hate on me player," Vikkas chuckled.

"Stop please, you are making my stomach hurt right now. Cameron is looking at me like I've lost my mind."

Tapping his fingers on the desk, he said, "Look I called to check on the updates for Milan's security system at the center. She's getting more traffic and I want to make sure they are all as safe as possible."

Shifting to a more serious tone, Daron assured him that all was going as planned. The updates would be completed within a week providing an unnerving sense of calm before all the impending chaos.

After disconnecting the call, Vikkas made sure that the file he'd been working on was saved. He shut down the computer, making sure everything was locked up in his office. On his way home, he decided to stop at the local market and pick up a bouquet of fresh flowers for Milan.

Arriving at his destination, he went to see his favorite florist. He called Ms. Branson in advance and she had a combination of two dozen red and ivory roses prepared for him. Baby breath and greenery accented the beautiful bouquet. He left after a few minutes of talking.

"Hey baby, I'm home," Vikkas said, walking through the front door.

Steak, baked potatoes, and string beans filled his nostrils with a savory aroma. "Hi, honey, I'm in here finishing up dinner," Milan replied.

"Um, it smells good," he said, as his footsteps echoed while heading in her direction.

Walking into the kitchen, Vikkas watched as his wife's smile brightened the space. Closing the space between them, he gave her the bouquet of flowers nestled in his hand. Leaning down, he laid a passionate kiss on her lips.

Looking into his eyes, Milan asked, "Is everything okay, baby?"

"Yes, all is perfect, my love."

"Okay, dinner will be ready in a few. Would you like something to drink?"

"No, I'm good right now." Smiling, he planted a tender kiss on her lips and laid the bouquet on the wine cart.

"I'm going to put these in water for you. Let me put my briefcase down and change into some comfortable clothes."

"Sounds good."

Turning around, Vikkas headed to his home office. Placing his briefcase on the black leather loveseat, he picked up the envelope laying on the corner of his desk. It was addressed to him but didn't contain a return address. Deciding to open it later, he placed it back down and went to change.

Twenty minutes later, the couple were enjoying their dinner. Sharing stories about each of their days. When they were done eating, he ushered Milan into the living room so he could take care of the dishes.

After her cooking a delicious meal and being attentive to him, it was his intent to return the favor. After cleaning up the kitchen, he fixed them each a glass of wine and went into the living room. Sitting down on the couch next to Milan, Vikkas placed his arms around her shoulder while the television played softly in the background.

Light breathing from his wife indicated that she'd fallen asleep. Holding her for a few minutes more, he enjoyed the feel of her presence. Kissing her forehead, he closed his eyes and an overwhelming peace surrounded him.

Carrying his wife to the bedroom, Vikkas laid her down and covered her up. He knew she was exhausted from working so hard on the upcoming expansion of the center and the influx of new residents. Everything seemed to be going well, in spite of the opposition they were dealing with. Tonight, he would rest well knowing that she was safe.

Chapter 15

Stretching, Milan rolled over in her comfortable bed and looked at the nightstand clock. It was 2:30 a.m. and she was wide awake. Looking to her left, she realized Vikkas wasn't next to her. That man was always up doing something.

She admired his tenacity, but worried that he might be doing too much. Spreading himself too thin. Milan wanted her husband around for a long while, so much time had been wasted with them being apart. They had a lot of memories to make and legacies to create together.

Freshening up, after getting out of bed, she set off to find Vikkas. He could only be one of two places, in his home office or out on the balcony. That man's brain was working overtime. Maybe, it was time for a pleasurable distraction.

No sign of him in the office, but sure enough she spotted him through the rear balcony doors. Standing still, for a few minutes, Milan studied her handsome man. He ignited something within her soul, mind and body that was unlike anything she ever experienced in life.

"Baby, why don't you just come outside and stop ogling me," Vikkas' rich baritone sounded.

Walking towards her husband, Milan asked, "How did you know I was standing nearby?"

Gently grabbing her hands and pulling her into his lap, he simply said "I always know when you are within reach, my love."

She looked into his mesmerizing eyes and leaned in for a sensuous kiss. It lasted for a few minutes and would have made unsuspecting bystanders blush uncontrollably. The air surrounding them was intoxicating.

Arching his eyebrow and speaking in a husky tone, Vikkas asked, "Why don't we take this inside?"

"What if I don't want to go inside?" Milan replied seductively.

Her husband began softly singing the lyrics to Maxwell's "whenever, wherever, whatever."

Standing up and holding out her hand, she simply said, "let's go." No other words were spoken.

Four hours later Milan stirred, happily gazing over at the peaceful face asleep next to her. Although they'd only been slumbering for a short time, she felt refreshed and rejuvenated. Good loving had that affect.

Her blissfulness was interrupted by the ringing of the telephone. She'd forgotten to place it on silent for a bit. Looking at the caller ID, her brother's name flashed across the screen and she sent it to voicemail.

"Why is this asshole calling me?" she thought to herself.

No love was lost between them. After the stunt that he pulled at the Chicago center, which ended up with her putting a bullet in his leg, they didn't have much to talk about. He'd also been warned by several of the Kings to stay away from her.

No sooner had she rejected that call, the phone was ringing again. As quietly as possible, she climbed out of bed putting on her silk robe. Walking out onto their private terrace, she reluctantly answered the phone.

"What the hell do you want?" Milan answered in an irritated voice.

"Hello Sis, what's good with you?" Seth asked.

"You have about ten seconds and I'm hanging up this phone."

Sounding wounded, he said, "Well damn, it's like that huh?"

"I don't have time for your foolishness, goodbye."

Before she could disconnect the call, her brother screamed, "Wait! Mom is in the hospital. You need to come home."

"And why would I do that?"

"Milan, she is not doing well. We don't know if she is going to be alive much longer."

A lot of time had passed, and she wasn't in communication with the woman who birthed her. Their relationship never recovered from the time Milan began staying with her grandaunt. She'd always showed respect and as much restraint as possible, but a ton of damage had been done to their relationship.

"Why should I care about that?" she asked quietly.

"She is your mother, Milan. What the hell do you mean?" he shouted in the phone.

"We don't get along and none of you have ever cared to check on me. So, why now?"

"Look, at the end of the day we are still family. We have one mother. I'm sure there are things you'd like to talk about before she dies."

She would never consider listening to anything coming out of this jail bird's mouth; however, this was a different situation. Even though her dysfunctional family wasn't heavily involved in her life, she felt a pull to make the trip. Milan did have questions that she wanted answered. She'd have to think about this and desired to talk it through with Vikkas.

"I'm not going to make any promises. Send me the hospital information. I'll be back in touch."

"Okay, Milan. I won't push, but know I think you should make this trip. I'll let you go."

"Yep, goodbye," she hung up quick.

Feeling as if the wind was knocked out of her lungs, Milan looked out across the horizon. She wasn't ready to wake her husband up, so she headed to the bathroom. Closing her eyes, she enjoyed the warm water from the rain shower head. A pair of strong arms surrounded Milan's mid-section startling her. However, she quickly relaxed against Vikkas' sculpted body while he placed light kisses along her shoulders.

"Why are you taking a shower without me, my love?" he asked.

Turning to face him, she said, "You were resting, and I didn't want to disturb you."

"Really, Milan?" Vikkas laughed. "I'm a light sleeper, you know that."

She had a feeling that he had heard the conversation with her brother. He was giving her the opportunity to talk about it. If she didn't choose this moment to do so, then it would come up later. Failing to meet his eyes, Milan held on to him tightly as a steamy mist of water rained down on them.

After a few seconds, Vikkas asked, "Baby, what is it? Who was on the phone?"

"I knew you were going to ask me that. It was Seth and I don't want to talk about it right now," she answered.

Lifting her chin, he looked into her eyes. "Okay, my love. But we are going to talk about this. You know I don't like to see you upset."

"Fine. Right now, I think you owe me a morning kiss."

"Really? I think I'll give you a morning kiss and a little bonus." Vikkas kissed her senseless, making good on his promise. A temporary distraction is what she needed, and her Adonis would oblige.

Chapter 16

After getting dressed, the couple went down to make breakfast and talk about the reason Seth contacted her. Vikkas knew his wife was clearly upset by the phone call. He'd give Milan a few minutes to get her thoughts together.

They sat down to a delicious meal of southwestern omelets, sliced fruit, and freshly squeezed orange juice. Not too much talking happened while the couple ate. It was a comfortable silence. As soon as the dishes were gathered up and placed in the dishwasher, Milan allowed Vikkas to lead her into the living room.

Taking a deep breath, she shared what her brother told her during their brief phone call. Her husband listened, while keeping her hands enclosed in his as a form of sharing strength. Tears began streaming down her face.

He watched as she wrestled with her thoughts. For these few seconds, he knew that she needed silent support. Giving her a moment to process what she was feeling.

"Baby, it's okay if you are sad about what is happening with your mother," Vikkas said. "I know her behavior towards you has been messed up, from an early age. But it's fine to have empathy for this situation."

"She doesn't deserve that from me," Milan whispered. "Why should I even care?"

"Because that woman is your mother. God choose her to bring you into this world and that was a gift. It's on her that she didn't cherish or act right towards you. But it doesn't change the lifetime connection between the two of you."

His wife didn't respond. Patience was one of his strong characteristics. Knowing her all of these years, Vikkas was able to gauge when it was time to speak.

After a few minutes, when Milan had chosen to be quiet again, he said, "we can call the hospital and check on your mother's current status. As much as I'd like to believe Seth is being straight with you about this, we need to check things out before making any plans."

"I would hope that my wayward brother is being up front with me," she replied. "I agree that we need to know all the facts before making reservations."

"Okay, sweetheart. Let's contact some folks and then we'll go from there. Are you ready to do that?"

Welcoming his sweet kiss, Milan shook her head that she was ready to make the necessary calls. She wasn't surprised about not hearing from any of her other siblings. Those relationships were strained a long time ago.

Prior to them getting married, Vikkas laid down the law with her family members. Many of them knew what happened with Seth and they didn't want a similar outcome. Besides that, everyone was well aware of the Castle and the men who were in charge. Foolishness and recklessness were not tolerated, especially when it came to those under their protection.

As the couple headed to his home office, he trailed behind in order to make a phone call to Daron. He made sure their discussion was brief, but informative. Knowing that the tech savvy guru would check everything and everyone out in Chicago made him feel at ease. No way they'd take the word of Seth alone. He'd proven that he was not to be trusted.

It bothered Vikkas to watch Milan stare blankly at the wall. He knew that she was struggling with her emotions. Who wouldn't be? Milan's mother had created so much strife in her life. He thought about all the insults, at least the ones that he knew about, aimed at them both. That woman was a piece of work, not much unlike the one who was trying to be a substitute for his biological mother.

"Hey, beautiful, are you ready to make those calls?" he asked.

Taking a deep breath, she replied nonchalantly, "sure."

Stretching his arms out, Vikkas motioned for his wife. "Come here, my love."

He provided the strength that she needed, wrapping her tightly in his arms. Most of the time his wife was a formidable force. Strong, mighty, and fearless, but she needed this connection with him.

"Okay, baby, I'm ready to make those calls," Milan said.

Her husband held her at arm's length. Looking into her eyes, as always, he wanted to make sure that she was being honest. Vikkas' discernment was something to behold.

"Alright, my love, let's get this done."

After making phone calls and verifying the information that Seth gave Milan, the couple had confirmation that her brother was telling the truth. At least this time. Now, it was time for Milan to decide what she wanted to do. He would support her if she wanted to travel to Chicago or decided against it.

She asked him for some space to clear her head. He decided to go visit with his brother, Jai, and sent a text to Cameron. She was one of trusted women in his wife's life and thought it would be helpful for them to talk. He'd deal with any consequences from his actions later.

Two hours later, Vikkas returned home to be with Milan. He needed to see her and wanted to know what she had decided to do. Cameron was leaving as he pulled up to the house.

His wife was sitting on the living room couch. As soon as he got near her, she exhaled a deep breath and tears began to form behind her eyelids. Vikkas sat beside her and pulled her into his chest.

"Talk to me, my love," he said in a soothing tone.

"I'm thinking about Momma Dee and what I promised her I would do," Milan shared. "I feel like I've failed by cutting my mother off all these years."

"Milan, you did the best that you could, and no one blames you for keeping a distance." Vikkas did his best not to sound angry. That woman was the part of the cause for their years of separation.

"I think I need to make the trip to Chicago," she said.

Making sure that he heard her right, Vikkas asked, "are you planning on going back to the states by yourself?"

Loosening his hold so that she could sit up, Milan looked him in the eyes and said, "yes."

Vikkas was speechless, a little disappointed, and concerned. He wasn't sure that she should be traveling by herself right now. If there wasn't so much going on, he would feel okay. Realizing who he was married to, he knew that he couldn't stop her from making the decision to go by herself.

Chapter 17

Milan couldn't understand why her wayward brother was so insistent about her coming back to Chicago to see their mother after all this time. That relationship has been strained for years. Resentment and unfair treatment plagued mother and daughter. Now, she found herself on a private jet heading to see the one person who caused nothing but strife in her life.

Vikkas wanted to travel with her, but she convinced him to stay in Durabia. She was clear about how apprehensive he was about her traveling solo with everything going on; however, she was determined to do so. After a heated discussion, he finally gave in and didn't fight her about it anymore.

She did her best to reassure him that everything would be fine. One saving grace was that some of the Kings, Knights and Queens were in Chicago. If anything went wrong, then help would be within her reach. In addition to the fact that her trusted steel companion was a Smith & Wesson pistol along with the tracker earrings that Milan conveniently forgot to wear at times.

After this trip, she didn't plan on going back to Chicago for a long time. Her main focus was gaining closure about things that only her mother had the answers to. She also didn't want to have any regrets when her mother transitioned. Death was a final and there wouldn't be a chance to deal with anything that needed to be hashed out between them.

Something felt off about this trip, but Milan shrugged it off. When her mind was set on something, she went full steam ahead. It was part of her DNA to not back down. No matter what.

Her flight took about 15 hours, but she managed to get some sleep. Perks of traveling on a non-commercial, custom designed jet was access to a luxury bedroom and bathroom. She had privacy and time to clear her head.

Engrossed in her thoughts about how the interaction with her mother would go, she was startled when the flight attendant buzzed back to let her know breakfast was ready. Soon after, the pilot informed her that landing preparation would happen in about thirty minutes. Taking a deep breath, she finished applying her makeup then headed out to the main cabin area.

"Thank you for the breakfast, Sarah," Milan said. She enjoyed smoked salmon, avocado toast, fresh fruit, and orange juice. It was all courtesy of her thoughtful husband who wanted to make sure that she had all of her favorite travel foods on the flight.

"You're very welcome, Mrs. Germaine," the flight attendant replied politely.

As they got buckled in and prepared for landing, Milan thought about walking into her grandaunt's home after all this time. She had hired someone to keep it expertly maintained for her. Daunting as it was to be back in the city, her heart felt at ease about being able to walk into the house that meant so much.

Milan's transportation was waiting and ready for her arrival. Her driver had the physique of a special operator, and she wouldn't be surprised if that was the case since Vikkas finalized her travel plans. That man was such a control freak, and his reach was worldwide.

"Hello, Mrs. Germaine, how are you today?" he asked.

Smoothing her hand down her purse and feeling for the imprint of her gun, she responded, "I'm doing well, thank you."

"My name is Steven McKnight and I'll be one of your personal chauffeurs during the duration of your stay her in Chicago."

"Chauffeurs?" she asked, receiving a slight smile in response. "That's good to know."

"Yes, ma'am. You will meet my partner when we get to your final destination."

After closing the car door and placing her luggage in the truck, he climbed into the driver's seat. "Are we heading straight to your grandaunt's house? Or do you need to stop somewhere else first ma'am?"

Laughing, she said, "you don't have to call me ma'am, I'm not an old lady. And, yes, that's where we are heading."

"That damn husband of mine," she thought. It was amusing and annoying that Steven already had an itinerary for her. She didn't fool herself into thinking Vikkas wasn't going to be thorough. With all of the drama and events that had ensued at the Castle, she knew better than anyone to believe there wouldn't be watchful eyes all around her.

This life was part of what she signed up for when taking those vows. All of the Castle men were dominant in nature and fiercely protected those who they loved. No holds barred. As suffocating as that seemed at times, it came with the territory.

Looking out the window, Milan observed the heavy traffic on the Chicago Skyway. Always busy and everyone in a hurry. She was glad that someone else had to navigate through this mayhem. Since they had about travel for about thirty minutes, she leaned her head back and closed her eyes.

"Mrs. Germaine, we are ten minutes away from the house," Steven said.

Glancing down at the key in her hand, Milan reflected on all the time spent there with Momma Dee. That woman loved her fiercely and she felt the same. It was unfortunate that her mother and siblings tried to get her to sell the house left in her name. Their motivation was nothing but greed.

Her husband made sure that they couldn't touch it. Her grandaunt's home stayed protected and safe. A privacy fence, swing gate and state of the art security system had been added courtesy of Daron Kincade, King of Morgan Park. No one would be able to sneak around, near or in the house. When the car came to a stop in the front of the residence, she noticed a man similar to Steven in height and muscular body type waiting outside by the entrance.

Milan watched as Steven exited the vehicle. He greeted the man with a firm handshake. Both of them looked in her direction when she opened the car door to get out. Turning towards her, Steven made the introduction that she'd been patiently waiting for. "Mrs. Germaine, this is Thomas McGraw. He is your second driver and will be riding with us beginning tomorrow."

Assessing him, Milan held out her hand and said, "it's nice to meet you."

"Likewise, ma'am," he said with a smile.

"Here we go with the ma'am," she laughed. "Gentlemen, I know that the two of you are more than drivers. I'm married to a man who has protection high on his list when it comes to those he loves."

Sharing a look between each other, neither man responded. Smirking, she walked past them and headed into the house. As soon as Milan closed the door, she took a deep breath.

Steven and Thomas gave her a few minutes alone when she entered the home. Taking it quiet ambience, Milan closed her eyes and stood in the living room. A few minutes later her bags were brought in and placed in the master bedroom. The men made sure she settled in, had their contact information, and let her know that they would switch off throughout the night with security checks.

The refrigerator has been stocked with her favorite foods, so she fixed a quick dinner then went to take a shower. Her phone rang and she smiled seeing Vikkas' name pop up on video chat. His handsome face put a huge smile on Milan's face. His sexy, quiet storm voice sent sensations to places that she wished he could reach out to touch. After finishing the call, she turned on the TV, but her mind flashed back to years earlier.

Chapter 18

"How did I get stuck with these people? Did I do something to make God mad?"

Milan replayed these two questions in her mind daily. For a fifteen-year-old, those were loaded questions that weighed down her spirit. Her teenage years should have been fun filled and carefree, but stress and anger were what filled those days.

Choosing your family isn't a personal decision. It's divinely ordained, at least that's the story shared throughout generations.

A combination of the twilight zone meets groundhog day was Milan's daily experience. Her days and nights were filled with emotional and mental abuse. All courtesy of the laser sharp lips housed by the woman who gave birth to her. Harsh, soul depleting words stayed engraved in her mind.

"You ain't no better than anybody else. You will never be anything important. Those books don't make you smart or hanging out with that white boy. He doesn't want you nor does anyone else."

Insults upon insults were poured upon her like a thunderstorm. Thunder, lightning then the non-stop downpour. She was the only one, out of seven children, humiliated and ridiculed.

"Just look at yourself, you ain't nothing to write home about. You're just a waste of air and space."

Milan's mother was an unhappy, bitter woman. Pearline Jackson had a house full of children she couldn't afford to take care of - five girls and two boys. She kept choosing men whose primary home was surrounded by electric barb wire. Orange jumpsuits were their primary dress code.

Government assistance provided the support that she didn't receive from her children's fathers.

Frustration and bitterness fueled her daily life. She treated her youngest daughter horribly. A switch went off every time Milan walked into the same room. Passive aggressiveness rose up, then came the nastiness and unsavory name calling.

"Where the hell have you been?" Pearline's venomous tone sounded as she inhaled the nicotine from her cigarette then took a drink of her alcoholic drink.

"Momma', I went to the library. I told you that I have that research paper due in four weeks for my English class," Milan quietly responded.

"I don't remember you telling me nothing about no damn library. Where are you hanging out with that white boy?"

"His name is Vikkas and he's East Indian. No, I was not hanging out with him today. I went to the library to work on my paper."

Pearline looked intently at Milan, convinced that she was telling her a bold-faced lie.

"I don't believe you. Why couldn't you work on your paper at home?"

"There are too many people in this house, and I don't want to fail my class. We don't have a computer here and I needed access to one."

"Maybe we would have a computer here if your no good daddy wasn't locked up."

"How is that my fault? You are the one who chose him, and I didn't ask to be born."

"What the hell did you just say to me?"

"You're always blaming me for him being a jailbird. I didn't choose that man, you did."

Pearline jumped up from the living room table with the quickness of a track star. Standing squarely in Milan's face, she said "I am so sick of your smart-ass mouth. Since you are so grown, grab your shit and get out of my house."

Milan looked at her siblings as they snickered and sneered at her. Without speaking and holding in the tears that were threatening to fall, she went upstairs to grab her birth certificate, social security card, learner's permit, and stashed emergency cash.

Milan's saving grace was her grandaunt. Mama Delores, known as

"*Mama Dee,*" in the neighborhood, was her trusted advisor and biggest cheerleader. Constant prayers and weekly sleepovers kept their bond unbreakable since her grandmother's death.

On a Saturday evening, they sat in the cozy, Afrocentric themed living room of her grandaunt's four bedroom, three-and-a-half-bathroom ranch style home. There were brown, beige, and burgundy hues throughout this particular space. Mama Delores had simplistic taste when it came to decorating.

Her head rested in Mama Dee's lap as Milan shared her innermost thoughts about the treatment, she faced living in her mother's house. This was her safe place. Transparency and honesty filled up the walls of this house, without the fear of being chastised.

"*Mama Dee, I don't understand why mommy treats me like that. She doesn't act that way with my brothers and sisters,*" she sniffled trying to hold back her emotions.

Her grandaunt lifted her head, looking into her eyes and said, "*Baby, your mama is my niece, but I know she ain't right. She's made some bad choices in her life and don't listen to nobody. You are something special and don't you forget that.*"

The onset of tears filled Milan's hazel eyes. She loved her grandaunt fiercely, feeling blessed that she had her to turn to. Clouds lifted and demons fled in this wise woman's presence. Being kicked out of her mother's house was hurtful, but it opened the door for her to stay with Mama Dee.

Gently holding Milan's face in her protective hands, she smiled and said, "I'm gonna' make sure you are alright as long as I'm breathing. Keep working hard and don't mind them folks trying to make you think less of yourself. You hear me?"

"*Yes ma'am,*" Milan smiled. "*I love you Mama Dee.*"

"*And I love you baby girl. Don't you ever forget that.*"

"*I won't. I promise.*"

"*Now, let's get some food in you.*"

"*You know Salisbury steak, mashed potatoes and green beans are my favorite, right?*" she smiled.

"*Girl, anything that I cook is your favorite,*" Mama Dee laughed. "*Go wash your face and hands then we'll eat. By the way, we're having your favorite dessert.*"

"Homemade apple pie and vanilla ice cream, can't wait."

"You are the best Mama Dee. Thanks for loving me the way that you do. I don't know what I'd do without you."

"Get, go do what I told you so that we can eat," Mama Dee said with wetness filling her eyes. She loved her youngest grandniece fiercely. Their tight bond was one envied by her own niece, and other grandnieces and grandnephews.

They had dinner then washed the dishes together. Time was now winding down to go to bed. All of the lights were turned out in the house, except for the one over the stove. Doors were double checked and alarm set. Hugs and kisses were exchanged as they settled in for the night.

Milan's room at her grandaunt's house was a couple of doors down. A purple and silver comforter set adorned the queen size, mahogany sleigh bed. Two nightstands and a matching dresser filled space in the room. It had its own bathroom, so she wouldn't have to use the guest bathroom in the hallway.

Being away from the chaos at her mother's house provided Milan peace. No antagonistic siblings to deal with or being blamed for something that had nothing to do with her. She could concentrate on school while feeling protected. A welcome change until the day Mama Dee took her last breath.

Chapter 19

Waking up the next morning, Milan prayed, showered, and ate a light breakfast. An eerie feeling overcame her as she entered the hospital. Steven and Thomas were already posted outside, ready to take her to the hospital. Milan already talked with Vikkas because they never let too many hours pass without connecting. The time difference didn't matter.

Forty-five minutes later, Milan was walking into the hospital. Mentally preparing herself for what she'd see upon entering her mother's room. It hurt her to feel this way, but nothing could change the damage that had been done.

Taking a deep breath and placing her hand on the doorknob, she took the steps needed to enter the room. Speechless, Milan looked over at the woman lying motionless in the hospital bed who appeared to be much smaller. Growing up, the petite brown skinned woman used to seem larger than life. A lot of that had to do with her mean streak and evil ways. Now, she appeared feeble.

"What is wrong with me? This woman doesn't give a damn about me. Why am I even here? Milan's empathetic nature surfaced, but she was doing her best to temper it.

Hatred and anger, the two emotions she felt because of the mistreatment and abandonment. Even when Milan tried to be respectful, it didn't matter to her mother. The way this woman acted towards her did not reflect the behavior of someone that is supposed to nurture and protect you.

"Mrs. Germaine, the doctor will be in shortly with an update on your mother," the registered nurse on duty told her. "Is there anything that I can get for you?"

"No, I'm fine. Thank you for letting me know," she replied.

"You're very welcome. Just hit the call button if you do need anything."

Shaking her head in response, she looked at her mother. Realizing this whole scenario was a little difficult, the intensity of the moment invoked all kinds of feelings. On one hand, she felt this woman was getting repaid for all the emotional abuse and internal scars that Milan endured. Then the compassionate area of her soul that wasn't tainted felt sadness.

Keeping a level head through this process was her intention. She thought about stepping out and making a call to Vikkas. Part of her wished that she didn't make a big deal about traveling back to Chicago alone. That man wanted to support her, but her stubbornness won. Now, here she was dealing with all of this emotional baggage by herself.

Lost deep in thought, Milan didn't hear when the primary physician entered the area. Startled by his deep baritone, she turned around swiftly.

"Hello, Mrs. Germaine. I'm Doctor Gibson," he smiled. "My apologies, I didn't mean to scare you."

"No worries, I should have been paying more attention," she said.

"You looked like you were deep in thought. I do that quite often."

Quickly gathering her thoughts, Milan asked, "what can you tell me about my mother's condition?"

"Your mother has been diagnosed with stage four lung cancer. Unfortunately, her years of excessive tobacco and alcohol use plus minimal physical activity contributed to where we are now. She has refused chemotherapy and any other recommended medications."

Looking over at her mother's weak body, she inquired, "how much longer does she have to live?" Seth wasn't a wealth of information and had chosen to be as scarce as possible. Her other siblings weren't anywhere to be found.

"Honestly, we didn't expect her to still be alive. It seems that she's been holding on for some reason. Maybe that reason is you," Dr. Gibson replied. "We are doing everything to make her as comfortable as possible."

"I understand and appreciate everything that you all are doing for her." In speaking further with the doctor, Milan understood that her mother was heavily medicated but should wake up in a few hours and be able to communicate. In the meantime, she decided that getting some fresh air was a necessity.

Surrounded by the sterile, cold environment of the hospital was not a comforting place for Milan. It brought back memories of her grandaunt being here before taking her last breath. Now, she was here for a woman who she despised, but was supposed to love.

She sent a text to Steven to let him know that she'd be coming out and wanted to go get something to eat. Ironically, he and Thomas had been sitting outside in the waiting room. They'd been given specific orders not to be too far from her.

Silently, they walked to the car garage. Both men were quiet and watchful, while she was thinking about the upcoming conversation with her mother. She'd listen to what the woman had to tell her. It was her goal to leave Chicago with a clear conscience.

As soon as Milan was situated in the car, her phone started ringing. Vikkas knew when she needed him. He was so intuitive, it was beyond scary. She often worried if he possessed some kind of magical telepathic gift.

Answering with a smile on her face, "Hi, honey, how are you?"

"Hello, my love. How are you?"

"I think I asked you that first," she laughed.

"I'm good now that I hear your voice, baby."

"You just say the sweetest things. I'm okay." Hearing Vikkas take a silent, deep breath, she knew that he was concerned about her.

"Just okay, beautiful?" he asked calmly.

"I will admit, this isn't the easiest thing I've had to do," Milan said. "I don't regret coming here and honestly, by the looks of things she doesn't have much longer."

"Baby, I'm..." he began.

"It's okay. If I need you to hop on a plane, I promise I will tell you. Besides, I think you have everything under control here since Steven and Thomas are glued to my hip," she chuckled.

"They better not be glued, because that would be too close. I would hate to have to replace both of them."

"Really, Vikkas?"

"Really, Milan? You know I don't play when it comes to anyone I love, and you are at the top of that list."

She knew he meant that from the depths of his heart. No debate when it came to her fierce warrior. He'd moved heaven and earth to make sure she was okay. His agape love nourished her soul.

Chapter 20

A couple of hours later, Milan watched as the green leaves swayed from the wind gusts while she was being driven back to the hospital. Light jazz music was playing in the background, while not a lot of conversation was going on. She knew both men were being polite and respectful of the fact that she needed this time to get herself together mentally. Speaking with her mother was not going to be a pleasant experience.

After her talk with Vikkas, she was fine. Hoping for the best and coming to terms, in advance, with the outcome of the discussion. Despite this being an uncomfortable moment, Milan was prepared to face whatever revelations about her life were shared. Also, she decided that this trip would be cut short as well. Originally, planning to stay for three weeks, she decided that wasn't going to be the case.

It was time to go home to her husband and life in Durabia. She planned on sharing the news with her husband later on in the evening. Milan knew he'd be happy to hear that since Vikkas wasn't too keen on her being in Chicago without him.

Finally arriving at the hospital, she calmed her rising anxiety by briefly closing her eyes and exhaling deeply. Steven and Thomas stepped out of the car to give her a moment to compose herself, then Milan let them know that she was ready to make the trek to Pearline's room. Upon entering, she was startled by the presence of her brother Seth. He'd been keeping his distance, so Milan assumed that he wouldn't make an appearance until she was close to leaving or gone.

"Hey Lani," he greeted her as if they were old friends. His eyes moved over his sister's shoulder, so she knew he spotted the men towering behind her. Without turning around, she was pretty sure that the look on her bodyguard's faces weren't welcoming to her brother. No doubt in her mind that Vikkas had put them on alert about Seth.

"What are you doing here?" she asked.

"Well damn, this is our mother," he responded. "Am I not allowed to be here?"

Milan looked at him, knowing that he was looking for a confrontation. She wasn't in the mood and wouldn't entertain his foolishness. It was always a game of wits with him, although he didn't possess any of those. Turning around to look at Steven and Thomas, Milan told them that she was okay. After a brief hesitance, they walked out the door. She knew they would stay close, just in case.

"Seth, you haven't been around since I arrived back in Chicago," she said. "So, why show up now?"

"Look, I've had things to do. I already knew you were here but was giving you time to spend with momma."

Chills ran down Milan's spine when Seth made that reference. She hadn't called this woman that for a very long time. It was unsettling to hear that term of endearment, especially with a heart that broken into pieces. Coughing made both of them turn towards the bed.

Weakened brown eyes settled over both of them. Surprisingly, her frail hand reached out for her daughter, not her wayward son. Taken aback, Milan stood still and didn't move forward at first. It took her a few seconds to get her bearings. Mama Dee came to mind, propelling her to take the necessary steps and grabbing a hold of the outstretched hand.

"Son, give me some time with your sister," Pearline said. Her request came out in a whisper, but her children could understand her clearly. She wanted to speak with Milan alone.

"Momma', maybe you should rest and talk later," her brother interjected. It was suspicious to Milan that Seth was trying to stop their mother from having a conversation with her. *"What is this fool trying to do now?"* she thought to herself.

"And maybe you should get up out of this room," she said. "I may be sick, but I know what I'm asking."

Milan's brother looked confused and bothered. However, he elected not to protest. There would probably be some heated words exchanged later between them. Reluctantly, Seth kissed their mother's forehead and left the room silently.

"Can you please help me sit up?" her mother asked, moving the attention back to her youngest daughter.

"Are you sure that's okay?" Milan asked in a cautious tone.

Huffing and weakly rolling her eyes, Pearline started to reach over and began pushing buttons on the hospital bed herself. Quickly closing the distance, Milan stopped her mother's movements and began helping her to adjust her position. She watched for any type of pain wrenching signs in case the nurse's call button had to be pushed.

"Thank you. Will you please grab a seat and come sit close so we can talk?"

"Okay," Milan agreed.

Now, it appeared that the time for them to discuss a few things had arrived. She hadn't planned on pressing her mother to open up. Divine intervention seemed to fall into her favor. Before they began talking, Milan helped her take a few sips of water.

Once Milan was settled back in her seat, she watched as her mother slowly rubbed her frail looking hands together. After seeming to have gained her composure, Pearline looked over at her daughter and began apologizing for the pain she'd caused over the years.

"Milan, I'm so sorry for my behavior towards you," she began. "It's not the way a mother should treat their child."

"Pearline, why now?" Milan asked, trying to keep the bitterness that she felt at bay. This conversation was too important to her. It was long overdue and she wanted to remain calm even though the anger was threatening to surface.

Looking at her hands and trying to hold back tears that were on the verge of falling, her mother said, "you were a constant reminder of how I messed up in life."

"What exactly do you mean by that, Pearline? The choices you made were yours alone. They had nothing to do with the fact that you made the decision to give birth to me." Pausing to take a deep breath, Milan continued, "Are you trying to tell me that I was a mistake?"

Pearline's shameful eyes met her youngest daughter's. "No, Milan. You were not a mistake." Finally, she allowed the tears to stream down her face and said, "I was so angry, bitter and regretted that I pushed your father away. Not letting him know about our beautiful baby girl."

Finally, the moment of truth arrived when Pearline revealed that Milan's father was living in Deepridge, South Carolina. He was married with two children, retired from the military and a successful entrepreneur. She'd been lied to for years about who her father was and the revelation left her speechless.

Anger etched on her face, Milan looked at her mother in disbelief and utter disgust. "Why would you lie to me about this?" she asked through gritted teeth.

"I was ashamed and hurt. When I found out that I was pregnant with you, he was getting ready to deploy overseas and decided to get married to a woman that he'd been involved with in South Carolina."

"So, are you telling me that he was dating you and this other woman?"

"Milan, I already knew he was involved with her. One minute they were on, then the next off. Raymond never lied to me, but I wasn't honest with him about my life."

Pearline shared that it was the one relationship she regretted damaging. They had started off as friends, but decided to cross that line. All of the bad choices and dishonesty caused Milan to be without her real father and deal with a lot of unnecessary strife throughout life.

"Baby Girl, there are no excuses for what I've done. I'd like to make this right while I still can. I know how to contact Raymond, do you want to reach out to him?" her mother whispered.

Chapter 21

Shocked and upset, Milan was trying to digest the information she received from Pearline about her biological father. His full name was Raymond Christopher Harriston. As soon as she'd gotten back to her grandaunt's house, she called her husband and the tears flowed as she shared the news with him.

Vikkas listened as she poured out her heart about the revelation. Milan was grateful for his patience and willingness to help her get more information. It was her intention to reach out and make the trip to Deepridge, South Carolina.

A few days later, she had her father's contact information. Gathering up the courage to make the call was not an easy task. She was unsure about the reception that she'd receive from him and his family. Fortunate enough, Milan didn't let that stop her from taking the first step of connecting with him.

After three rings, even though it seemed as if minutes had passed, a baritone voice answered the phone, "Hello."

"Hi. May I speak with Raymond Harriston, please?" Milan asked.

"Speaking, how can I help you?"

Taking a quick deep breath, she said, "my name is Milan Germaine. By chance, do you remember Pearline Jackson from Chicago?"

Silence

"Are you still there, Mr. Harriston?"

"Yes, I'm here. Give me just one moment," he replied.

Heavy footsteps sounded and then a door closed signaling that he had been on the move as Milan waited patiently for him to continue their call.

"Okay, Milan. I have more privacy now," Raymond said. "I think you'd better start from the beginning. Who are you?"

"Pearline is my mother and that would make me your daughter," she said.

Explaining who she was seemed awkward, but her father didn't discount anything that was shared. He continued speaking with her over the phone and shared his desire to meet her in person. Milan told him the reason behind her being in Chicago, Pearline's illness, and promised to arrange a trip to South Carolina in the next few days.

Vikkas let her know that he'd be making the trip to the states and wasn't listening to any of her opposition. Until then, he asked her to keep Steven and Thomas in the loop.

"Milan, promise me that you will not travel by yourself to South Carolina," Vikkas said.

"Baby, I won't do that. Even if I wanted to, my two bodyguards would not give me the space or time to ditch them."

"That's because they were special operators in the military and are getting paid a lot to keep you safe."

"I understand. Please stop worrying okay," she said.

"My love, I will always be concerned about you."

With her mother's condition worsening, she decided to make the trip sooner than planned. Vikkas' travel plans were delayed because they had an incident at the center that he decided not to share with her. Jonathan has been caught trying to access confidential files and was being detained. When she told him about her plans, he was not happy. Milan tried to diffuse the situation by letting him know Steven and Thomas would be traveling with her.

After letting her mother's physician know that she'd be out of town for a few days, Milan and her bodyguards boarded the private jet. As soon as they landed, a car was waiting for them to pick up. A lake house had been rented for them to stay in for the next few days and it would be the location for the initial meeting with her father.

Twenty-four hours later, Milan was looking into the face that was a blueprint for and mirror of herself. Skin tone, eye color and their assessing demeanor were reflective of each other. This was the man that helped to create her, although he didn't get the opportunity to raise her.

Words seemed to escape them both as they sat looking at each other. Trying to figure out the right words to say. Many years had passed, and they had the opportunity robbed from them to form a father and daughter relationship. If it had not been for her mother's selfishness, then this scenario would look a whole lot different.

Speaking up, Raymond began the conversation telling her the condensed version of his journey from Chicago to South Carolina. Sharing how he met her mother and a little about their whirlwind relationship. He also talked about what made him become an entrepreneur. As time passed, he asked Milan questions about her upbringing and where she was in life now.

She told him about her living with Momma Dee. They also discussed her broken relationship with Pearline. Then talked about her husband Vikkas and how they met one another. Spending almost a day together, they had lunch brought in as well as an early dinner. It was surprising to both the ease of them relating to one another and openness of conversation.

"I'm glad that you came, and we had this chance to talk," Raymond said.

"I feel the same and I look forward to meeting everyone tomorrow."

"Now, I can't promise this will be an easy interaction with them. But I will do my best to ensure that they understand you and I will be working to build our relationship."

"I appreciate that," Milan said. "Thank you for being available to spend this time with me." She watched as a sincere smile crossed her father's face. Feeling encouraged that this was the start of something special.

Chapter 22

Waking up the next morning, Milan was well rested and energized. After taking a shower and getting dressed, she fixed breakfast for herself, Steven, and Thomas. Suspecting they had already been up and doing security checks, that was the least Milan felt that she could do.

On cue, the duo walked into the kitchen. "Good morning, Mrs. Germaine. What time would you like to leave today?" Steven asked.

"Good morning, gentlemen. We can discuss that once we're done with breakfast. Here's your plates," she said. Handing it to them, she noticed their apprehension and smiled. "It's okay for you to eat with me. If my husband was here, he'd be eating with us too."

After a few seconds, they each took a plate and sat at the counter. In unison, they said, "thank you, ma'am."

"You're welcome. And once again, please stop calling me ma'am," she laughed. They ate in a comfortable silence, then she cleared the dishes when they were finished. Milan let Steven and Thomas know that once she spoke with Vikkas then she'd be ready to leave the lake house.

An hour and a half later, they were on their way to her biological father Raymond's house. No more than ten miles into the ride, Steven began looking in the rearview mirror and quickly glanced over at Thomas whose weapon appeared in his lap. "I think we are being followed," he said smoothly. "Whatever you do, don't turn around. Remain calm and follow our lead, Mrs. Germaine."

Inhaling then exhaling, Milan said, "okay." She didn't ask any questions. Trusting their instincts, she knew they were trained for these types of situations. They'd been around each other for a couple of weeks and both men took this job seriously. They'd already mapped out different routes that could be taken, despite the fact they were in a rural area. Milan placed her hand inside her purse, making sure that her gun was within reach. While she had come to value Steven and Thomas, they were also aware of her expert marksmanship.

Turning on one of the alternate routes, Steven was prepared to speed up as Thomas kept an eye on the trailing vehicle. Suddenly, a thin mist of vapors was released through the ventilation system. Coughing and trying to catch his breath, Thomas said, "what the hell?"

By the time, they tried closing them it was too late. As the car slowed both men were becoming disoriented. Steven told Milan, "when this car stops, get out and run."

"What is happening? I can't leave you here to get hurt," she said. Now, looking back she noticed the car following them had slowed to a crawl. Eerily creeping towards them with four occupants.

"Listen to him, Milan. We need you to run," Thomas chimed in, struggling to stay alert while Steven mustered up energy to get the car stopped safely.

Looking out the windows, Milan noticed that they were surrounded by corn fields on both sides of the road. All she had to do was make a dash for it and try to get lost so she'd be able to call for help.

Taking her heels off, she leaned over the seat and checked for pulses. Steven and Thomas were breathing but knocked out cold. Milan felt herself starting to succumb to the vapors, but she was a fighter and planned to make a run for it. The other vehicle was getting closer, so it was now or never.

Grabbing her gun and managing to get the door open in the process, she rolled out coughing. Trying to catch her breath and gain her composure, Milan got to her feet and took off. Her body swayed as she dashed into the corn field just before the other vehicle stopped.

"Hurry up and find her," the familiar voice sounded.

"Are you kidding me? It can't be him," Milan thought to herself as her legs caved and both knees sank into the soil. Listening intently, she crawled determined to buy enough time so that maybe someone would

drive pass and stop to see what was happening.

As quietly as possible, without making her location known to the men, she willed herself to keep moving forward. Milan's progress was halted in an instant when a pair of jean clad legs appeared before her. She looked up into the face of Seth.

"What the hell are you doing here?"

Milan fought to aim her gun at his chest but her arm wasn't cooperating. It felt like her limbs were falling asleep.

"Don't worry about it, you'll find out soon enough," he snickered. Seth leaned over and placed a cloth over her nose and mouth, then picked her up, causing her to loosen her grip on the weapon. Milan's world went pitch black.

Chapter 23

As the fogginess wore off, Milan's eyes began to open. Moaning and holding her aching head, she took a little time to sit up on the bed she'd been placed in. Unsure of what drug had been used, she was trying to shake off the aftereffects and become aware of her surroundings.

"Where am I?" she asked out loud.

Trying to remember what happened was exhausting. She took a deep breath and worked on getting her bearings while fighting off being disoriented.

Standing up at a snail's pace, Milan's focus began to clear. She took in the furnishings decorating the room. Looking around, she noticed everything in the room reflected someone with lots of money. King size bed, cherry wood dresser and nightstands, custom rug, and high-end abstract art on the walls.

"When did kidnappers start living a lavish lifestyle?" she thought to herself. *"How long do they think I'll be here?"*

Baffled and confused, she began to wonder who the mastermind behind this abduction was. No doubt, her brother was involved, but he wasn't the smartest criminal. Milan knew a substantial amount of money had to be the main reason for his deception. In addition to the fact that he wanted revenge for being shot.

"I have got to figure out my location," she whispered to herself.

Milan began to focus on the nearby sounds. Not knowing how much time she'd have alone, it was important to pick up on some type of clues. Not sure if there were cameras in the room, she tried to be discrete with her movements. Nothing sudden, just slow, and steady.

One window facing what appeared to be the rear of house had security bars over it. Cherry wood blinds covered the interior, but they were left slightly open. Burgundy curtains were hung matching the bedding that was accented with blue and gold.

Crickets chirped nearby while there appeared to be a body of water in the vicinity as well. Stream, lake, pond? Prompting her to believe that she was located somewhere rural.

"Could I still be in South Carolina?" she asked herself. As she was pondering this question, the room door swung open.

"I see that you're awake. Did you get some great rest?" Varsha asked. Her face was void of any real concern. Behind her stood a huge bodyguard. A towering, familiar presence – *Thomas. What the hell?*

Milan's poker face was in place. As angry as she was, it wouldn't be smart for her to attempt any bold moves until it was clear what she'd be dealing with. Standing by the window, she looked between Varsha and one of the men that was hired to protect her.

"Well, dear, are you speechless?" she sneered. "It's unusual for you to be this quiet."

"What exactly are you looking for me to say?" Milan responded.

"You must be wondering why you are here, with me."

"Right now, Varsha, I'm really not in the mood to play these games with you. There are a lot of things running through my mind at this moment."

Letting out an evil laugh, Varsha said, "you may not want to play now but I would recommend that you get ready darling. Reckoning day is here and you all are going to pay. So, get comfortable and enjoy the ride."

Milan studied the woman's expression and elected not to respond. Normally, she'd give a verbal spanking to anyone who was disrespectful to her. In this moment, she was still reeling from the fact that Varsha would go to these lengths because of the hatred as well as to get even with Khalil and her own son. What kind of monster does that?

"Since you seem to be unable to speak, I will leave you with your thoughts. Hope you enjoy your current accommodations because they will be changing for the worse soon enough." Varsha looked at Milan from head to toe, then sashayed out the door with Thomas trailing close behind. Momentarily, he glanced back before the locks were engaged on the door.

Milan was still in shock, but not surprised, that shameless woman was involved with this whole fiasco. Thomas was an even bigger shocker. Varsha was a heartless woman, and her bitterness wouldn't allow her to see Vikkas happy with someone who wasn't from their culture. Thinking back to high school, Milan remembered the fake smiles and hostile sideway glances that Varsha gave her many times.

Upon reconnecting with Vikkas, at the insistence of his father, it was evident that woman's attitude hadn't changed. *In the private hospital's waiting room, Varsha had the nerve to be insulting and rude while demanding to know why Milan was there. Khalil had been shot and that should have been the focus, but it wasn't for the former Mrs. Germaine. In a swift manner, Vikkas let Varsha know that she would respect Milan because that is who he chose to be with for life.* The look that evil woman gave her was very telling about the challenges she'd be facing moving forward.

A person with no morals was capable of anything. Everyone should have known better than to underestimate Varsha considering she tried unsuccessfully to drug Khalil in order to get pregnant. Milan knew that she needed to be prepared to fight her way out of this current situation. Even knowing that her husband and their castle family would be devising a rescue plan, she would be figuring a way out as well.

Chapter 24

Watching Vikkas and Jai talking through the glass patio door of the rented house, Khalil said a silent prayer for his daughter-in-law. It warmed his heart that the brother's bond continued to grow stronger. As he pivoted to look around at the Kings, Knights and Queens working overtime to connect the dots and find Milan, his soul filled with pride and admiration.

His years of mentoring and providing support for them had been fulfilling. They continued to exceed his expectations. Now, they rallied together to take care of one of their own as the group continued to do. Without hesitation or any questions.

"We have to find my wife," Vikkas' baritone sounded thunderously. All movement halted for a few seconds. Everyone knew that he was in pain, but they had to stay focused and push all emotions to the back burner. He looked up as his father walked out on the patio towards them.

"Son, Milan is going to be found safe and sound. That woman is intelligent and fearless. Don't doubt that she isn't trying to find a way back home to you."

"Father is right," Jai added. "Your wife is a very resourceful woman. As hard as we are working, I know that Milan is doing the same to make sure she is back at your side."

Glassy, distraught eyes looked back at them. Tears didn't fall, but they were right on the cusp. The weight of not knowing his wife's current location was heavy. On top of finding out that Varsha was involved. He tried his best to show that woman respect, in spite of herself, and this is how he was repaid.

Vikkas' usual strong demeanor and composure were shattered. Fear to murderous were the levels of emotions that he was battling. Along with the feeling of helplessness that was unfamiliar to him. Khalil's arms wrapped around his shoulders, then led him into the kitchen. Jai followed closely behind to provide another layer of support.

He was determined that his wife would be found and brought back home safely. No matter what obstacles had to be moved out of the way. And all of those involved would pay, in blood if it came to the point.

The Castle family were all working together and overtime to locate Milan. Using all necessary resources and doing some recon on Varsha along with her sorry excuse of a brother. Vikkas and everyone knew that she was in South Carolina but hadn't pinpointed her exact location. The tracker on her gun had a strong signal and provided them with information in the general area, but they didn't want to go in totally blind. Especially since there were a lot of wooded areas and unknown terrain that they have to contend with to launch the rescue.

Although Milan's relationship with her father was developing, Vikkas reached out to the man. Wanting to give him the benefit of the doubt that he was not involved in her abduction. Also, he wanted to find if her father really cared enough to assist them in the search. Only time would tell, and they'd go from there.

"You really need to eat something, son," Khalil said.

"I'm not hungry," his eldest son mumbled.

"Brother, keeping up your strength is important. What do you think Milan would say if she could see you now?" Jai asked.

Jumping up out of the chair and within inches of his brother's face, he squared off. His nostrils were flaring, and he resembled an angry bull. Every mention of his wife's name seemed to feed his temper.

"Vikkas, stop this now! What the hell is wrong with you?" Cameron shouted. Daron was standing a few steps behind protectively with his hand on one of her arms.

His head whipped around. After looking at the concern on her face, he began to calm down. He had allowed his despair to get the best of him. Taking it out on the people who loved them and were doing their best to find Milan.

Looking back at his brother, he said, "I apologize, Jai. I shouldn't have done that." He noticed that his father stood quiet.

"It's all good, I have tough skin. Just know that we are here to help every step of the way. We love Milan too."

Running his hand through silky hair, Vikkas did a panoramic view of everyone in the kitchen. His eyes landed on Cameron, and he said, "this is hard and cuts deep on so many levels. I'm really sorry for being an ass." Releasing a deep exhale, he sat and didn't say anything else.

Chapter 25

Looking blankly at the ceiling, Vikkas was trying to fight off his fatigue. His brother, Jai, convinced him to go to lie down for a little bit while everyone worked through the current leads. His anger, frustration and adrenaline were high. With Milan missing, peace would not come until she was back in his arms.

He knew that he had to take care of himself in order to have his strength when it was time to go rescue her. For now, he would try to take a quick rest then get back in the midst of the search. Managing to fall into a deep sleep, Vikkas began to dream about the day Milan became his wife.

Happiness coursed through his veins while looking at the woman of his dreams walking toward him. The taupe beauty who captivated his soul deeply was being escorted down the aisle by his father, Khalil. That wise man knew Vikkas belonged with Milan and kept tabs on her while the couple were separated for years.

The radiance bouncing off of his bride brightened every step that she took toward him. He took in her curvy stature fitted in a strapless, ivory wedding dress. The bodice was accented with gold crystals matching her tiara and veil. Vikkas was thinking about the quickest way to get her out of that dress as soon as they were alone.

Tears began to fill his eyes as his heart was beating at a rapid pace. He felt his brother and best man, Jai, place a calming hand on his shoulder. As Milan got closer to him, he took in her beautiful face and the smile that emerged on her lips. The day had arrived for them to become one.

"Wake up, brother, we have a lead. It's time to go," Jai's voice woke Vikkas out of his slumber.

His eyes opened quick, and he looked around to make sure that this wasn't a dream. Sure enough, his brother was waiting with patience as Vikkas got his bearings. Staring wide-eyed at Jai, he asked, "did you say there is a lead?"

"Yes, time to get yourself together and then we need to roll." His brother did an about face and high-tailed it out of the room.

In one swift movement, he jumped out of bed and went into the bathroom to freshen up. Entering the living room, Vikkas felt as if he was in grand central station. He watched as gear and computers were being placed in bags. Immobilized by the hurried pace of everyone.

"Son, are you alright?" Khalil asked. He hadn't realized that his father was standing next to him.

"Maybe a little sleep deprived, but I'm good. Jai told me that we have a lead."

"Indeed, we have an exact location. Thanks to Seth."

"Come again?" Vikkas' eyes turned into slits.

Turning to his left, one of the faces that he didn't expect to see appeared. His quickness, despite the lingering fatigue, allowed him to reach the intended target within seconds. Before anyone could react, his fist connected hard with Seth's face.

"What the hell, man?" he screamed in pain. "I came to help because I know where she is, but Lani won't be there much longer."

"Where is my wife?" Vikkas roared. Daron and Jai grabbed him as he was prepared to make connection again. Cameron appeared, blocking his view.

"Look, you can kick his ass later. I'll help you," she said. "We know where Milan is being held and it's time to go get her. Are you ready to do this?"

As angry as he was, that seemed to do the trick. "Let me go, I'm good," Vikkas said in a calmer tone. Both men looked at him to make sure that was the case. Right now, they needed to focus on getting to Milan as quick as possible.

Pointing at Seth, he said, "I'll deal with you later and you better hope that nothing has happened to my wife.

Chapter 26

Knowing her time was running out, Milan was doing her best to find a way to escape from the house. As much as she tried being nice to the bodyguards, it was obvious their loyalties to Varsha were strong. They made sure nothing left around could be used as a weapon against them.

Her nemesis boosted about the fact that she had prepared contingency plans to make sure they couldn't be found right away. When she had asked about Seth, Varsha became agitated and swore that he would pay for his deception. She received word that he'd gone rogue, which probably meant that he went to provide information to Vikkas and Khalil.

Laughing, Milan wasn't surprised that he used the clueless woman to get paid, then flipped on her. Venomously, Varsha looked at her and said, "things won't be comical for you much longer" and walked out.

Pacing around the room, Milan looked at the clock. She was told that she'd been scheduled to be transported in four hours. The evil woman had the nerve to gloat about the fact that she was having her shipped off to Nadaum.

Looking out the window, she whispered, "Baby, if you can hear me, I need your strength right now."

As soon as the words escaped her lips, a loud boom sounded and the smell of smoke entered her nostrils. The lights flickered off and all hell broke loose in a matter of seconds. Curses, screams and gunshots rang out. She anticipated that it was a matter of time before someone came rushing through the door. However, Milan wasn't sure who it would be, so she braced herself to face whoever.

Her fighter's instinct was strong, and she didn't mind doing a little hand to hand combat. Those Krav Maga lessons would pay off, although she would have preferred a gun, but there wasn't one in sight. Looking up towards the ceiling, she muttered, "Vikkas, I love you."

Seconds later, the room door burst open and Milan ran full speed towards the person. No one was taking her to be tortured. She'd die fighting for her freedom.

"Milan, it's me!" Cameron shouted, holding her arms in place. Then she spoke into an earpiece, "We've got her and we're heading your way."

Inhaling then exhaling a deep breath, she looked into the face of her gladiator friend. Milan hugged her tightly after the grip was loosened on her arms and looked behind Cameron to find Daron. He was keeping watch on the corridor and glancing back to make sure they were ready to move.

"It's good to see you, but we've got to go. Here take this and anyone that looks hostile, shot them." Cameron handed her a 9MM Glock with the safety disengaged.

Blinking, Milan was relieved that Cameron and Daron were there helping to rescue her.

"Hey, girl, you with me? We gotta' go."

Taking a deep breath, "yes, I'm good. Lead the way out. It's good to see you both."

Daron acknowledged Milan's statement with a quick head nod. "Let's move, ladies. Shoot first, ask questions later."

Making progress down the stairs and through the lower level of the house, the King of Morgan Park was bringing up the rear as they made their way towards the exit. They encountered several hostiles. As bullets buzzed by them, the two Queens held their own quickly eliminating a majority of the threats. Both of the women were expert shooters. *"Where is Vikkas?"* Milan thought to herself but didn't voice it because she needed to focus on the task at hand - freedom.

Movement in her peripheral caused Milan to glance over and see Varsha trying to escape through a side door. Cameron and Daron were right behind her as she took off in the opposite direction to catch the woman that caused all of this mayhem. A few yards from the door, Thomas stepped into view causing the trio to slow down in their tracks.

"Move," Milan shouted, her body visibly shaking.

"I can't do that," he said.

Raising her gun, she calmly repeated the command. The only response she received was movement of his head side to side and then a roll of his shoulders. Thomas was ready to do battle and she'd make this fight a quick one.

Without speaking a word and with the quickness of a cheetah, Milan pulled the trigger and shot him in both legs. He fell to the floor with a loud thud.

"I told you to move," she said.

"You handled him," Cameron nodded at Thomas. "And we'll take care of them."

Milan glanced back to see four men approaching seconds before more gunfire erupted.

Without a backward glance, she ran out of the side door to try and catch up with Varsha. Hoping that she hadn't gotten far.

As soon as she made it outside, Milan spotted Vikkas. He was standing with Jai and Khalil who formed a human barrier between him and Varsha. She was sporting handcuffs courtesy of the call made by Aashna after they stopped her from getting away. Putting the safety on her weapon, she ran straight into her husband's waiting arms.

"My love, I am so glad to see you," he said, holding her snugly.

"Baby, I happy to see you too," she said, as tears began to flow down her face.

Everyone stood in a protective stance around the couple. In the background, Varsha kept raging on about this not being over. Aashna, who had made the trip to help in the rescue efforts, had enough. She walked over to the woman and slapped her face leaving an imprint. "Stay away from my family, you evil witch."

Stunned into silence, no one said a word. Khalil and Jai looked in the other direction.

Looking into her husband's face, Milan wanted to see if he was bothered by what just happened. He didn't even comment. Police statements were taken at the scene, and they asked everyone to be available for any additional questions.

Milan and Vikkas headed to the lake house. A new security detail was with them. Steven had to be hospitalized but was expected to be discharged in a day. When they got there, Milan's father Raymond was waiting. He told her that he needed to make sure that she was okay for himself. They hugged and made plans to get together soon. She appreciated Vikkas giving her that moment with Raymond. Now, she turned her focus to him.

Chapter 27

Shifting in bed, Vikkas turned to where Milan's body should have been resting. Placing his hand on the empty space, his eyes immediately popped open. Sitting up ramrod straight, he looked around but no trace of her. A simmering amount of panic began to set in.

Jumping out of bed, clothed only in black silk boxers, he checked the bathroom. His heart began to race, she wasn't in there. After the craziness they'd been through with Varsha, her brother and those who conspired to take his wife away from him, Vikkas was still on edge. In reality, he knew she had to be somewhere in the house; however, his subconscious made him feel the opposite.

They'd made the trip back to Chicago because Pearline's health had deteriorated. Despite the ordeal that his wife had been through, Milan wanted to be there for her mother. Instead of staying at Momma Dee's house, they were at their home in Wilmette.

Walking in a hurried pace to the living room, his eyes immediately zoned in on the couch. His wife's silhouette came into focus. Tightly wrapped up in a purple throw, Milan appeared to be sleeping soundly. Dim lighting in the area was provided courtesy of the muted television.

Breathing a sigh of relief, Vikkas sat by her. His hands traced her face and the outline of her body in a delicate fashion, confirming that she was there in the flesh. It may have seemed like a silly action, but one that he felt was necessary. They both had been dealing with the emotional and mental scars from her abduction. Being unable to sleep comfortably was one of those effects for Milan.

His wife was a light sleeper, but she didn't move or flinch. Exhaustion seemed to have taken its toll on her body. Listening to her light breathing, he closed his eyes and gave silent thanks that she was safe in their home. "I love you, baby," he whispered, while placing a light kiss on her forehead. He wanted to move her back to the bed, but this was the first time she seemed to be resting. Every time Milan had a restless night, since being at home, she'd head to the living room.

Deciding to let her remain where she was, Vikkas went back to bedroom and grabbed himself two pillows and a blanket. Choosing to lie in front of the couch, so he could stay close to his wife and be there when she woke up. Wherever his queen was settled, that is where he desired to be. The floor being uncomfortable was the last thing on his mind.

After a few hours of sleep, Vikkas stirred and opened his eyes in a leisure fashion. They looked into the face of his beautiful wife, who was stretched out next to him on the floor. It was a pleasant surprise for him.

Smiling, Milan said, "Good morning."

"Morning, my love," his deep, smooth voice sounded.

"Baby, why are you on the living room floor?" she asked.

"Because you were out here on the couch and I wanted to be near," Vikkas shared.

He welcomed the soft kiss that she planted on him. It warmed his heart that his wife was captivated by the way that he loved her. Snuggling in each other's arms, they didn't make a move to do anything else.

"What would you like to do today, my love?" Vikkas asked, after a few minutes of silence.

"I'd like to stay right here," Milan responded softly. "Unless the hospital calls us and we have to go there."

Thirty minutes later, they remained wrapped in the cover up on the floor. Both of their phones were on silent while they embraced the quietness of the house. As much as Vikkas enjoyed being around everyone, he was happy to have this time alone with his wife.

After getting up to shower and eat, Vikkas suggested that they put on lounging clothes and just chill. However, his father and mother had other plans because they showed up on the couple's doorstep. That was the beginning of the trickle effect for the rest of their castle family to make appearances.

Keeping an eye on his wife, he wanted to make sure that she was doing okay with all of the unexpected company. He knew that they all had the best intentions and were concerned about Milan adjusting after her ordeal. Cameron had already put him on notice that she'd be checking on her in person often, while her childhood friend Pilar called, and video chatted frequently.

Walking over to where she sat with Cameron, Vikkas looked down at his wife and asked, "Hey, my love, are you doing okay?"

"I'm doing fine, baby," Milan said. "Go, talk with the guys."

Looking into her eyes, Vikkas received the silent confirmation that she was okay. He kissed her forehead, smiled at the other two women, and swaggered away.

"That man loves you and has got it bad," Cameron laughed.

"I know and tonight I am going to show him I have it bad for him too," she winked then looked in his direction.

As if on cue, Vikkas glanced back at his wife. She had that look in her eyes. It was going to be a great night, so he would have to hurry this impromptu get together along. These folks had to go home.

$$\mathcal{C}hapter\ 28$$

Three weeks later, the couple was back in Durabia. Her mother passed away five days after Milan's rescue. To her and Vikkas' surprise, Pearline had left some specific instructions with an attorney about how she wanted things handled upon her death. Her youngest daughter was designated as the executor of the will that she had drawn up a few years ago.

The ungrateful siblings that decided to show up after Pearline's death were angry. Promising to fight Milan every step of the way. Vikkas asked Shastra "Shaz" Bostwick, King of Evanston, to represent his queen during this process. Since Seth was in jail for an extended stay, all of the hell that they tried to raise was short-lived along with the will being deemed ironclad.

Waking up in her husband's arms, feeling safe and secure, Milan felt at peace. It took some time for her to start healing from the abduction. Vikkas had been so patient and gentle with her through this process. She knew that he was struggling just as much as she was since being back home. Both of them dealing with the anger and feeling of betrayal courtesy of Varsha and brother Seth.

Almost daily, the Kings, Knights and Queens took turns checking in on them. Khalil, Aashna, Jai, Temple, Daron, and Cameron all led the charge. As smothering as that seemed, she welcomed the love knowing there were people who genuinely cared about them. Realizing that sometimes the best folks who come into your life don't share your DNA.

Watching her husband's easy breathing and his relaxed, handsome face, Milan felt blessed. Overwhelming love filled her soul for this man. He was her king, lover, friend, and soulmate.

Her mind flashed to what their children would look like, how they would act and the joy their presence would bring in their lives. Milan's desire to become a mother had grown. She planned on sharing her thoughts with Vikkas. Experiencing firsthand how fragile life could be, it prompted her mindset to shift.

"Good morning, my love," her husband's husky voice sounded. "How are you feeling?"

"Good morning, handsome," she smiled.

"Having a good night of sleep will do that for you."

"Well, if I recall, we did more than sleep last night," Milan replied seductively.

Vikkas' eyes turned molten. The physical connection they shared last night was nothing short of fireworks. Explosive and powerful.

After a few weeks of individual and couple's therapy, their communication grew stronger, and they didn't avoid talking about what happened. Milan was open about her fears, regrets, and self-blame. Her husband was just as honest about his feelings, and they were able to begin moving forward from the aftermath.

"What would you like to do today, beautiful?" Vikkas asked.

Smiling and looking adoringly at her husband, "I think I'd love to make a baby with you, then we can figure out what to do the rest of the day."

Rendered speechless, he gazed deeply into her eyes asking, "Are you ready for that, my love?"

"Yes. I am so ready to start our family. That's if you are, baby," she replied. "With all that we've been through, I don't want to waste any more time or delay starting on this journey with you."

"Creating lives that represent the love we share," he started, "would be one of the greatest blessings, my queen."

Running her fingers through his hair then a hand down his muscular chest, Milan said, "since we have to put in the work, then I think we need to get started."

"Your wish is my command, beautiful."

No other words were spoken. Only the sounds of sensual, toe-curling lovemaking. Each partner pleasurably giving as good as they got until sated.

Two hours later, the blissful couple were dressed and heading out to meet Jai, Daron, and their queens. Skipping breakfast, they decided to have an impromptu lunch together. Milan, Temple, and Cameron decided that they would eat at their favorite restaurant that served American and East Indian food.

Looking out of the passenger side window, Milan smiled as the inner joy reflected externally. In her peripheral, she saw her husband's sly grin as well. Happiness exuded from both of them. Not just from their earlier physical connection but overcoming the challenges of their ordeal.

"My love, what are you thinking?" Vikkas asked.

Turning her head to face him, she replied, "I'm sure it's the same thing that you've been smiling about."

"Um. Tell me what you believe has been on your man's mind."

"If I have to explain that, then obviously one of us is not doing something right," she smirked. Both of them laughed and Milan reached over to intertwine her hand with Vikkas'.

"Trust me, I think we broke some records last night and this morning."

Everything was getting back to a sense of normalcy. No more immediate threats to Milan or Second Chance Safe Haven because they'd been handled. Jonathan confessed about doing his best to keep tabs on Milan for Varsha because his mother's life had been threatened. He met the evil woman during one of her secret trips to the area where they lived as she was plotting and planning revenge.

Vikkas was ready to ask the Sheikh and Sheikha to exile the young man to Nadaum, but Milan stepped in. She felt he deserved a chance to redeem himself. His mother was safely brought to Durabia and they were provided shelter as well as jobs in the free zone under strict security watch. One wrong move and the current agreement would be null and void.

The King, Knights, and Queens worked hard to make sure all those involved were being punished with well-deserved jail time. Now, Milan could focus on expanding the center, getting to know her father and most important becoming a mother as she fulfilled the role of Queen of Wilmette. She didn't take that lightly and planned to be purposeful about it each and every day. It was as important as the Smith and Wesson that she never left home without.

ABOUT THE AUTHOR

U.M. Hiram is a #1 Bestselling Author, Book Coach, and Interior Book Designer. She is a human resource professional and retired Navy veteran, currently residing in Kansas. Her love for writing began at an early age, evolving into independent publishing.

She currently writes in multi genres that include Christian fiction, contemporary romance, paranormal, and romantic suspense.

Reading, traveling, watching sports and spending time with her family is what she enjoys doing the most when not putting pen to paper.

Website: https://authorumhiram.com/

Bookbub: https://bit.ly/UMHiramBookbub

Facebook: https://bit.ly/UMHiramFacebook

Goodreads: https://bit.ly/UMHiramGoodreads

Instagram: https://bit.ly/UMHiramInstagram

Twitter: http://bit.ly/AuthorUMHiram

Persistence: The Power & Breakthrough of Fervent Prayers
Book# 8 in the Merry Hearts Inspirational Series

At the age of nineteen, I found myself pregnant and unsure of what the future held. Plans definitely changed, I'd originally pictured myself as a performing artist, a successful singer and actor. I'd always wanted to be a mom; however, I didn't think it would be that soon in life. But when certain precautions aren't taken and you find yourself "in love," then the outcome is evident. That was probably one of the scariest times in my life.

Wrapping my head around the fact that I'd be responsible for this living, breathing little person who would depend on me for everything was such a daunting reality. So many thoughts raced through my mind about how I would provide for my child. I wasn't sure if I'd ever go back to college and finish out a degree program. For the time being, higher education was put on the back burner.

Growing up in the projects of New York, I didn't want that same reality for my child. Don't get me wrong, my sister and I didn't want for anything despite the fact my mother had to use government assistance. We always had a roof over our heads, clothes to wear, and food to eat. To be honest, we had no idea we'd been living as a low-income family. The main prayer prior to and after my son's birth was for me to be strong on this journey with him. I had seen how hard it was for my mother to navigate her way through motherhood without support from her husband. Unfortunately, their marriage faced some challenging times and they ended up separating while my sister and I were still young. One minute I had a father in the home, then in the blink of an eye that changed.

A change such as this has a huge impact on a child. As I look back over some of the decisions I've made in life, in particular when dealing with relationships, it's extremely eye-opening. Becoming a mother, especially at a young age, pushes you to embrace adulthood at a quicker pace. Now, I understand what "unconditional love" and selflessness truly mean. A maternal instinct kicks in and makes you look at life and the world a whole lot differently. Selfishness is placed at bay and your thoughts are shifted to the gift you've been given. This responsibility is very scary, joyful, unpredictable, and exhilarating. Being able to embrace this stage in my life and knowing there was a higher power at work helped in this transition.

I was going to be in a similar situation of raising a child minus the marriage, the same circumstance my mother had found herself in. And I would be much younger going through it. During my pregnancy, I was grateful for the fact that support came in the form of my son's godparents. Admittedly, the relationship with my mother was contentious because she was unhappy about me expecting a baby.

Needless to say, once Malcolm made his entrance into the world, the relationship between my mother and I began to heal. It's amazing how much of an impact this little person made on every adult he came in contact with. He melted hearts and brought so much joy to those around him on both sides of his family.

Providing for him was one of the main reasons I decided to join the military. It would provide a steady source of income. A significant part of that was the fact that my family was full of veterans who served in all of the different branches. Missing a few firsts for my baby boy was unthinkable, but the reward was going to be much higher than what I was going to be giving up. At least in my mind, it was.

The separation from him for a little while was extremely hard. Struggling with the guilt of having to leave Malcolm in the care of my mother bothered me a lot. He served as a huge source of motivation for me to successfully complete boot camp. I would not quit, no matter what I had to endure to get to the finish line.

The overall plan was for him to join me as soon as I'd gotten settled at my first duty station in Virginia. However, the time right before leaving for boot camp in Orlando was pure torture. The good thing for me was he was so young. Even though I missed him taking his first steps, it was a blessing he would be able to remember all the times with me after that. Asking God to sustain me through all of the transitions and milestones was consistent. Those fervent prayers brought an amazing village into my life. Malcolm became part of their families just as I did.

Finally

Michael's unnatural silence was unsettling. The same phone number kept popping up on his phone, but he chose to ignore the calls, which was strange. He'd been on the phone non-stop while heading to the airport, so another caller shouldn't have bothered him the way this one obviously did. Finally, he answered.

"Is there something that I can help you with?" he asked with an aggressive edge to his voice.

The caller's voice was inaudible because he had turned his face away from Michelle and the volume was lower than normal. He listened intently and didn't say much. It was obvious that Michael didn't appreciate the current conversation because he sat ramrod straight.

"Look, I'm not going to talk to you about this right now. I'm heading out of town and will be gone for a few days. I'll call you when I get back." He disconnected without another word.

Michelle glanced sideways at him. Tension filled the interior of the luxury limo, which had been pleasant and light just a few moments ago. Clasping his hand and lacing their fingers together seemed to break down the wall that had gone up when he answered the phone.

Michael knew it was a matter of time before Michelle questioned him, so she did away with the suspense. "Who was that, baby?"

"Nobody important, I'll deal with it next week."

"Are you sure about that? Things were okay before you took that call."

Michael's body language spoke volumes. He sat stiffly, staring through the window clearly done with the conversation.

She wouldn't push for answers. At least, not at this moment. She'd focus on the trip ahead. Besides, there were ways to take his mind off stressful people and situations.

After making it to the private terminal, their passports and luggage were checked seamlessly. By the time they boarded the jet, the tension rolling off Michael dissipated. The pilot, co-pilot, and flight attendant made sure everything was in place and ready for takeoff.

Once they reached flying altitude, Michael made a few phone calls to tie up some loose ends with business.

Michelle looked out at the beautiful blue backdrop as the opulent jet glided through calm skies. Engrossed in her thoughts, she didn't notice when Michael sat beside her.

"Hey, baby. A penny for your thoughts." His rich baritone vibrated in her ear.

"Just thinking about our trip and all the fun waiting for us."

Leaning back further into him, she closed her eyes as his muscular arms wrapped around her. They'd both been looking forward to this trip where there would be no interruptions from their hectic lives back in DC.

"Are you done with your phone calls?"

"Yes, ma'am, I'm all yours. We have lots of flight time left, so take a nap and I'll wake you when it's time to land."

"What if I'm not sleepy?" she said, while yawning. Her brain wanted to be naughty, but her body needed rest.

Michael laughed and kissed her on the forehead. "Sleep baby. I plan to keep you up all night, so you're gonna' need this time to relax."

"Um hmm" was the last phrase that escaped Michelle's lips.

Michael adjusted his position so they'd be comfortable on the plush sofa. Rosanna, their flight attendant, checked to make sure they didn't need anything. Michael placed a finger on his lips and motioned for her to close the privacy curtain until it was time to land.

Forty-five minutes later, they were on the way to their final destination. Excitement and anticipation hung in the air. This vacation was well overdue. When their rented villa came into view, the sight was breathtaking. Michelle sensed she would enjoy her time on the island.

"Welcome to Montego Bay, Jamaica, Mr. and Mrs. Daniels. My name is Armstrong Monticello. I'll be your personal concierge during your stay on our beautiful island."

The handsome young man standing just outside the doorway couldn't have been more than twenty-five years old. His blemish free skin, warm brown eyes, and Hollywood smile added to his sex appeal. Despite his attractiveness, Michelle only desired one man and was ready to be alone with him.

She didn't correct Armstrong about the greeting. Although she was ready to be Mrs. Daniels, that wasn't yet the case. Intervening, Michael thanked Armstrong for the warm welcome as the young man led them inside the villa.

While the bags were taken to the master suite, Michelle made a beeline to the massive terrace. The view of the vivid blue-green Caribbean sea was breathtaking. She closed her eyes and inhaled. The murmur of Michael's voice as he spoke with Armstrong filtered to Michelle where she stood.

A moment later, Michael stood behind her and rested both hands on her hips. "Alone at last. What shall we do?"

She turned in his arms, brushing up against his hard body. "I can think of a few things. Let's start with a hot shower."

"How hot do you want it?" he asked with lust-filled eyes.

"As hot as you can make it," she murmured.

With that, she gently removed his arms from around her body and stepped into the passage leading to the master suite. Pausing before she entered the huge space, she asked, "Are you coming?"

Wearing a devilish grin, he said, "Yes, and you will be shortly."

The water temperature was nothing compared to the heat generated while they showered together. Capturing a handful of her hair with one hand while the other gradually made its descent past her navel, Michael found the sweet spot that had Michelle moaning uncontrollably. The room filled with sounds of her pleasure.

Meanwhile, she stroked his manhood relentlessly, which made him hiss and curse. They were both building each other up to a huge climax. She sensed that Michael wasn't ready to be pushed over the edge, and she was right.

He quickly moved her hand and dropped to his knees. His tongue took the place of his fingers, where he had been delivering pleasure. In moments, Michelle grabbed his head and screamed his name as her back arched and her core exploded against his mouth.

Once she stopped shivering and her vision cleared, she looked down at him completely sated. He licked his lips, while holding her up. If he didn't, she would have fallen.